I0571255

CAMERON'S COURT

DANIEL AMORY

.

Copyright © 2011 All Rights Reserved.

About the Author

Daniel Amory, an award-winning writer, was born in Chicago, Illinois in 1975. He made his first foray into writing as a Staff Writer for *The Daily Cardinal* while in college at the University of Wisconsin-Madison. In the fall of 1998, he began to work professionally as a journalist in connection with *The New York Times Magazine*, *A&E Television* and *The History Channel*, producing numerous documentaries seen worldwide.

Daniel lives in Chicago with his wife, Jennifer. They are regular contributors to many community and philanthropic activities.

Visit Daniel Amory's Websites At:
Facebook:
http://www.facebook.com/profile.php?id=100001730901052#!/profile.php?id=100001730901052
Amazon:
http://www.amazon.com/DanielAmory/e/B004GFI3CW/ref=ntt_athr_dp_pel_pop_1
Twitter:
@danielamory
Blogspot:
http://danielamory.blogspot.com/

1

I suppose I should have known the food they were going to

serve at the holiday party was going to be terrible. I mean, it was in

the wonderful basement of the Mid-Town Inn restaurant after all.

Inside there was wall-to-wall carpet, a twelve gallon tropical fish

tank, bread bowls of stale-looking bread on tables, containers of

mismatched butter packets and coffee sweetners, uncomfortable

high backed chairs, gorgeously red painted walls and BBQ wings

that looked like they had been sitting there all morning. However, I was starving because I hadn't eaten breakfast so I didn't really care if the BBQ wings looked like they had been sitting there all morning. Nobody else seemed to be eating much, but I gobbled about two handfuls of the mild ones. You should have seen the way that Peter Galecki was plowing through them. I guess you can't complain about free food.

Along with the wings, there were soft pretzels and what looked to be like biscuit gravy. Galecki said it was cheese sauce. It was a cheese and artichoke sauce and the pretzels were just pieces of pretzel. They were cut up. It wasn't even the whole pretzel. There were also lukewarm quesadillas where the cheese wasn't melted anymore. The waiter—this guy—said to me, "Vegetarian quesadillas are on this plate and chicken is over here," pointing to a plate beside the vegetarian one. "If you like chicken, you've got to try this one," he added very enthusiastically. He was very enthusiastic, this guy, this waiter, and he was really pushing the chicken ones, so, what I did was I tried it and it was bland.

I hated coming to these things. Coming meant I had to smile and listen to everyone blame their problems on the economy. Recently, an e-mail had been sent and division-wide layoffs after the first of the year were inevitable. It was, for many, an indoctrination into the economic fallout of the new era of corporate greed that had been in the midst of giving a swift kick in the pants to America for the past year.

"If you look at the last fifteen years of us growing up, everything has been fake," started a lawyer I knew by sight to another lawyer I didn't know. "Wall Street and its big bonuses and Ponzi schemes, baseball players and steroids, child abuse cover-ups with priests; what do you have left if you don't have finances, sports or religion?"

As I stood there, I obsessed in generalities about my future and whenever I obsessed in generalities about my future I would think about Gatsby's schedule for self-improvement that Henry Gatz handed to Nick at the end of *The Great Gatsby*.

I looked over at Galecki, who was hunched over making chomping noises while gobbling the wings. It was depressing standing there watching Galecki gobble the wings the way he was gobbling them. I truly felt sorry for him and his overactive thyroid. But it was depressing. God was it depressing. I mean he chomped just like his dad. He chewed with his mouth open like his dad. As if watching Galecki eat his wings wasn't fascinating enough! We had to have the chomping noises! I thought back about the time he had invited me over to his parents' house for dinner. I remembered how his mother kept coming out with food. It was as if she made everything that night because she couldn't decide what to serve. I had never seen so much food nor two people more in a hurry to eat than Galecki and his dad. Here, they were making these glorious sucking and chomping noises with their mouths open while I was sitting there and his mother kept entering the room every ten minutes with another dish.

There are probably three things you should know about me before I go any further. First, my name is Cameron Hoffenberg.

Secondly, I'm a senior at Armitage High in Chicago. And, finally, third, whenever I read *Tropic of Cancer* by Henry Miller I have the courage to take on the world without exploding and I hadn't read *Tropic of Cancer* in awhile.

The basement was getting crowded. It was almost uncomfortably crowded. I guess the late arrivals hadn't heard that the party had been pushed up to 10:30 A.M. to cut costs. All around me there were lawyers and law clerks and paralegals from the State's Attorney's office. Some faces I recognized from my department, many I didn't. Galecki wasn't the loudest. Nick Masters was the loudest. He kept yelling everything from the top of his lungs. Justin was dancing. He was dancing to Michael Jackson with his winter coat on. He said he wanted to do the moonwalk. He was wearing a coat because his shirt was wrinkled. He said his cat slept on his shirt and wrinkled it. That's what he told me this morning after I told him he probably just picked it up off the floor in his bedroom.

Galecki kept making jokes about the Governor and Illinois politics and how corrupt it was and it was me and Galecki and Ethan and Nick and Justin and Steven and Tara for awhile. Steven, who was a Supervising Attorney, was just going along with Galecki, but after awhile he turned to him and said, "You should cool it with the political jokes." Galecki said, "Why should I cool it with the political jokes?" He did it very light-hearted and everything, but it was still awkward.

I walked back over to the buffet with the wings and started to eat some of the hot ones. The hot ones were so spicy my lips started to burn. I stood there eating the wings and feeling the burn on my lips and smelling the pretzel cheese sauce while carefully looking at the cheap ornaments decorating the fake Christmas tree. There was an Elvis Presley figurine riding a motorcycle that would spout *Viva Las Vegas* every time you pressed a button. It was exactly the kind of place that would have a fake Christmas tree with an Elvis Presley figurine riding a motorcycle.

"I'd be surprised if John's in next week," said an attorney with a big chin who worked down the hall from me. He was standing on the other side of the tree. I had only known the Elvis Presley figurine spouted *Viva Las Vegas* because he had pressed the button twice.

"You're not going in on the 24th, are you?" asked the attorney standing beside him.

"Nope," said the attorney with the big chin. "Monday and Tuesday next week. Monday and Tuesday the week after that."

As I worked on my second handful of wings, the rarely seen State's Attorney, James M. Dolan, and his stupendous hair, turned to me as he walked in the door and asked in passing, "Good wings?"

"Yeah," I said, automatically.

"Good," he said winking, then smiling toothily as in "I'm one of you."

It kind of reminded me of the smile Adam Schwartz, the head of the Green Acres Day Camp would flash for parents during

Parents' Day. Green Acres was one of the most popular camps in Chicago and I was a junior counselor there one summer and on Parents' Day they would bring in ponies for all of the kids to ride in order to make the parents think that the kids were always riding ponies. They would really bring in ponies for all of the kids to ride. It was sort of like an unspoken agreement between everyone, campers included, that even though everything that went on during Parents' Day was pretend we would act as if it were real. When the parents observed the pool, for instance, the campers were given swimming lessons from certified lifeguards instead of counselors and junior counselors, like myself, who would ordinarily be the ones giving the lessons. I mean, on an ordinary camp day, even if you were a terrible swimmer yourself, you'd be one of the ones giving the swimming lessons to the campers and the certified lifeguards would watch from the deck. I'm sure Adam Schwartz, the sneaky bastard, figured that the kids' parents would be interested in seeing that the certified lifeguards were the ones giving the lessons.

Anyway, Dolan smiled at me just like Adam Schwartz would smile at the parents and the thing about the wings being good and all was really the extent of our conversation. He brushed passed me and moved around the room, winking and nodding and patting backs. *The ass-lickers with their leader*, I started to think to myself. The masses were looking at him with great reverence. I remained boldly by the buffet as they postured for position around him. Through the years, I've always been able to stand my ground boldly. During my birth, I remained boldly in my mother's uterus for an extra ten days and through two false labors before finally having to be induced. My mother has a very artful way of telling this story and she always ends it by saying that my inducement was a foreshadowing of my personality.

I looked across the room at the ass-lickers. You should have seen the line that was forming. It was as if Dolan was a celebrity or something. It looked like Galecki was first in line. It figured. From everything I knew about Galecki, it figured. Galecki was a senior at Southport High and was in the Illinois State High School

Leaders Internship Program at the State's Attorney's Office with me that semester. The Internship Program, which lasted for ten weeks, was geared toward "exposing high school seniors to the daily operations of the State's Attorney's Office." Well, we saw the daily operations, all right. We both did together every day after school. We actually shared an office. Galecki was a little overweight, a little insecure, a little neurotic. Everything he did vaguely irritated me, but he was sort of likable. It was his saving grace.

Probably the best way to describe him to someone that didn't know him was to say that if you had by chance walked in on him in the bathroom when he was already in there alone, he was the kind of guy that would be leaning over a wet counter looking at his gorgeous chubby self so closely in the mirror you would think he was making love to it. I mean, there was this one day when I had spilled yogurt onto my desk and I walked into the bathroom down the hall to get some paper towels and Galecki was leaning over a wet counter and looking at himself so closely in the mirror you would think he was Frenching it with his tonsils. When he heard me walk inside, he quickly pretended to have something in his eye when I knew he had been squeezing out a whitehead.

You should also probably know that Galecki loved to talk about food. Food was something Galecki and I had in common though. We both could lightly philosophize about food for hours. But Galecki was more adventurous than I was when it came to actually trying different foods. He was like Columbus in that respect. He was truly a Columbus in a chubby, high school senior's body and I was an occasional philosopher of the seven food groups.

Anyway, that was Galecki; he liked to lean over wet counters and French mirrors while looking at his gorgeous self when he was in the bathroom alone, he was like Columbus when it came to trying different foods, and he would fight with the masses of ass-lickers to be the first one in line to shake Dolan's hand at an offbeat, red-walled office holiday party. Oh, and he liked to describe to me in excruciating detail for hours on end all the women he was supposedly hooking up with. Of course, they were always living in Canada or Ohio or something. All of Galecki's women were world travelers. It was never believable. For hours on end and it was never believable. I should also probably mention, in order to give the most accurate depiction of Galecki that I can, the fact that sometimes his pants were tight on him and his belt would buckle over and when we would be out picking up something to eat at this one place across from our office I would have to wait for him as he struggled to get his wallet out of his back pocket in front of the woman at the register. So, it was the unbelievable stories about the women he was supposedly hooking up with, the struggle at times with his wallet, his likeness to Columbus when it came to trying new foods, the Frenching and the ass-licking. That was essentially Galecki in a nutshell.

"They're all clock watchers," said the man in the dark suit behind me to a nodding head. "Nobody in my department is in before nine and nobody is there after five."

I stood there watching the line around Dolan mount. The gullibility of the crowd only rivaled its clock-watching and ass-licking ability. I bet it didn't make any difference at all who any of us were to a guy like Dolan. I imagined he considered himself to be a significantly superior bastard given the ass-licking going on in the room. I've actually never been a good ass-licker. However, even if I was the King of the ass-lickers, I doubt Dolan would have dared tried to shake my BBQ sauce caked hands with the hot sauce under my nails the way it was anyway. Part of me was glad for that. I stood there and watched Dolan work the room and as my lips started to burn from the wings, I slowly began to inch my way past the ass-lickers to the bathroom.

The same beautiful red color was on the walls in the bathroom as the rest of the basement. I leaned over the wet counter and pressed down on the soap dispenser. Somebody, I noticed, had discreetly written "Kilroy was here" in permanent black marker on the narrow band of red wall over the sink.

I examined my face in the mirror. As I wiped the BBQ sauce from my lips, I looked at the little scar above my eyebrow. It was basically a thin white line over my right eye now. You couldn't see it because it was couched in my eyebrow, but I knew it was there. I got it one winter long ago sledding with my father down the big hill in the park by our house. The sled had tipped over and I went head first into the metal fence that courted the bottom of the hill. I only knew that I was bleeding because the snow around me turned red. I remember my father rushing me in the car to the emergency room. I got six stitches that day and, in all honesty, I don't think I ever went sledding again.

All of a sudden, Dolan and his stupendous hair came barging in and stepped up to the urinal. He looked over his shoulder and saw me scrubbing the BBQ sauce from under my nails. His hair wasn't anything if it wasn't stupendous. It was common knowledge, of course, that it was a piece. I stared at it knowing it was a metaphoric clue, a guise, his guise, the perfect guise and a perfect symmetrical summation that lampooned his persona and a piece of present day America.

"You're the guy with the wings," he said, weaving at the urinal.

"Yeah," I said.

"They were good?" he asked, importantly.

"Yeah, they were good," I said.

"Good," he said.

If he was so interested in the godforsaken wings, why didn't he just try them himself, the pompous bastard, I thought to myself.

That's because he probably had lunch reservations at some expensive restaurant after making his appearance with us ("the riff-raff"). I guarantee you a guy like that had no qualms about pushing wings that were sitting out all morning at a dump like The Mid-Town Inn on us and then going to an expensive restaurant.

I kept reminding myself of the Fat Lady—the Fat Lady concept from *Franny & Zooey.* It was something I often had to remind myself about when I was around people like Dolan. The idea of the Fat Lady was that every person deserved respect regardless of how fake or dumb or egotistical they were and one was to imagine a Fat Lady to represent that person in one's mind. The problem was that Dolan was often the Fat Lady that I would think about when I would think of this Fat Lady and now he was standing ten feet from me.

As I went on scrubbing my hands, I started to realize that like Dolan, I was probably somebody's Fat Lady. In fact, I was probably Dolan's Fat Lady. Actually, I think I was probably the quintessential Dolan Fat Lady. It was probably for that reason, and that reason alone, he asked me about the wings not once, but twice. I was Dolan's Fat Lady. And he was mine. I was standing over a wet counter scrubbing BBQ sauce from under my fingernails and Dolan was a breadth of a shoulder behind me weaving at the urinal and we were mutually tolerating each other having just finished politely commenting about the wings even though we both knew how awful they were after having been sitting out all morning because we were each other's Fat Lady.

What I started to do next was to think back to the first time I saw Dolan. Not surprisingly, it involved a similar setting. It was an event during the first week of the Internship Program and he was, of course, schmoozing and he was the most charming and sophisticated fake bastard of the bunch.

"Excuse me, but I have to go to the little boy's room," I remember the very tanned and sharply dressed Dolan saying at the time with the same wide toothy smile to a couple of other tanned lawyers who all smiled widely with their teeth and talked and dressed and acted like one another.

Inside the bathroom, I remember after Dolan had finished tucking in his shirt and zipping up his pants at the urinal, he had walked over to the gold plated faucet and long marble sink top and like the kind of guy he was faked the washing of his hands. He then walked out into the dining room and laid a huge palm rubbing handshake on Arnie Schneiderman, who was sitting at a table with his wife, and all I could think about when he was slapping serious skin with Arnie was for Arnie to go wash his hands. Believe me, I tried to send Arnie a message through telepathy to go wash his hands but it didn't work because right after shaking Dolan's hand, Arnie ripped off a large piece from a roll, sculpted it with butter and ate it. And then he handed the other half to his wife.

I would have told Arnie and his wife to go wash their hands before eating the roll, but you can't tell someone to go wash his hands after shaking the hand of a terrific bastard like Dolan the way Arnie Schneiderman shook it. I mean, you should have seen the way Arnie Schneiderman shook Dolan's hand. He practically killed himself reaching for it over the table and silverware.

Anyway, as I presently stood inspecting my fingernails in the mirror of the bathroom at The Mid-Town Inn, I can't tell you that I didn't have any fleeting thoughts about introducing myself to Dolan. I mean the bastard was the State's Attorney and all, but there was something about the red walls in the bathroom and, well, I decided that I really didn't want to offer to shake hands with him weaving at the urinal the way he was so I kind of just left. It wasn't, of course, though, until after he gave me another socially awkward bathroom-type of fake smile with everyone of his teeth on my way out.

I walked out to the excitable ass-lickers, who were now hovering around the bathroom door. Dolan walked out a few seconds later and began addressing everyone amassing near the buffet in his most important voice.

"It's December, it's the holiday season, which, as you know outside, is the beginning of the time of the year that we say comes in like a lion and out like a lamb. Well, the lions are roaring."

He proceeded to follow up this pronouncement with a deep lion's roar. You should have seen him roar. He went on to thank the bureau for their hard work this year. At some point, he singled out all the interns and law clerks and told us that if we worked very hard one day we too could be the State's Attorney just like him. It was some horrible canned speech on par with everything else he had done that day, but the adrenalized ass-lickers applauded as if he had just given the Gettysburg Address anyway. After his wonderful speech, he bowed with the apology that he had to leave.

He then gave a few short politician waves to the crowd and a few more toothy smiles, and quickly exited with his stupendous helmet-looking mane stage right.

Soon thereafter I listened as one of the ass-lickers, an overweight woman in her mid-forties who was a paralegal in my division, tried to recall in a blighted attempt to the woman standing next to her what Dolan had said.

"In like a lamb, out like a lion."

She said it with the profound tone that JFK used when he said, "Don't ask what your country can do for you, but what you can do for your country."

I looked over at Galecki and watched as he finished off another handful of wings while ogling ravenously across the room at the Ice Princess as she slowly brought a glass of water to her mouth. Natalia, known as The Ice Princess to those of us in the office, was also in the Internship Program. Physically, she was tall and slender with long blond hair. She was originally from Ukraine and spoke little English—an added tidbit to the dream-like, coldness that made her forever the Ice Princess that she was. Galecki was in love with her, but she could only be loved from afar. Neither one of us had said anything outside of the occasional hello in the hallway to her in passing, but Galecki would get hysterical about her. I told him—I kept telling Galecki—'stop getting hysterical. She doesn't even understand what you are saying to her in your mumbles.' But it didn't matter what I said. He would get hysterical. All ten weeks he was hysterical.

I watched him absent-mindedly finish off another handful of the hot ones before I left. I left for no other reason than because I couldn't stand being there in that basement with the ass-licking and the posturing and the burning of my lips and the smell of the pretzel cheese sauce and the red walls and the fake Christmas tree with the Elvis Presley motorcycle figurine and the mismatched packets of butter and coffee sweetners and the sound of Galecki absent-mindedly gobbling the hot ones down by the handfuls while ogling ravenously at the Ice Princess anymore.

2

Outside it was snowing. I lowered my head and angled it at the gusting December wind as I stepped out onto the lush white uneven hint of the sidewalk with a herd of overcoats. On the corner there were sanitation workers spreading salt and plowing snow from the street. The sun disappeared into a low dense sky drooped with clouted gray clouds hiding the tops of tall buildings.

I waited at the intersection at the edge of a pool crystallizing into ice along the side of the street while a bus with fogged windows passed. As I crossed the street behind it, my feet carried snow from one street corner to the next. Chicago was one of the only cities where in the winter the streets felt empty and deserted and crowded at the same time. With my face becoming numb from the cold, I glanced at my watch and wondered whether I should see a movie because I had nothing better to do until my four-year-old niece Chloe's ballet recital later that night, and the story of that day really begins as I walked inside a coffee shop on Dearborn Street to warm-up from the dropping temperature.

As the ice crystals in my hair evaporated away in the line by the register, my ears slowly got their feeling back. At the counter, I poured a little cream into my cup and as the steam came forth, I heard someone call my name. I glanced over and saw Marty Feldman at a table near the fireplace. Marty was a real estate attorney and was my father's childhood friend.

"Your mother told me you were going to give me a call," said Marty, in his usual deep voice.

"Yes," I said, pausing slightly. "I've been meaning to."

"Do you have school today?" he asked, noticing I was blowing at the rim of my coffee like I had all the time in the world.

"We're on winter break," I said.

"Well, I have a few minutes now if you want to talk," he said, looking down at his watch.

"Um, yeah, sure," I said.

I sat down in the chair across from him, setting my coffee on the table as he moved some papers aside.

"So you're mother tells me you're going to college next fall and you're thinking about pre-law and are looking for some advice."

"Yes," I said, nodding.

"Well, you should know, pre-law and even law school doesn't prepare you to practice law," he said. "You learn on the go."

He made a small gesture with his hands.

"You will need to find someone that will teach you."

My eyes narrowed attentively.

"I don't have the temperament to be in litigation, if that's what you're interested in going into."

He paused for breath.

"If you haven't noticed, I'm a little impatient," he said with a slight smile. "And I have a temper."

He sat up a little straighter.

"When I had an argument in court, I would stay up all night thinking about it, re-playing it in my mind."

He looked closely at me.

"Basically, litigation is you piss on my head and I piss on yours and let's see who wins."

He hesitated for a moment.

"It's ugly," he said, raising his eyebrows for emphasis. "It's drawn out. The worst thing to do is actually litigation."

His eyes gradually moved about the coffee shop.

"I always tell my clients to settle," he said, his eyes resting on me. "I don't think there's been one time when I have had a client go into litigation and come away with everything they want."

He joined his hands together.

"Some of the best litigators I know can go into court and make their argument, piss on the other side and then come out of court and forget about it. They have short memories."

I nodded slightly.

"Actually, some of the best litigators I know are friends with the other side," he began again. "They can go get a beer together afterwards, after pissing on each other."

He drew his coffee to his mouth and sipped.

"If I had to do it all over again, to be completely honest with you, I think I would have gone into business."

He unlocked his hands and leaned back in his chair.

"With how hard I had to work, I would be a rich fucking bastard," he said after a thoughtful pause. "I'm much more entrepreneurial than working in a structured setting like your average billable hour attorney schmuck."

He smiled faintly.

"I've never been sold that this was the way for me. But I had a wife and a mortgage and three kids. I already had the handcuffs. The Golden handcuffs."

He bent forward and glanced at his watch.

"Well, listen, I have a Better Business Club of Greater Chicagoland meeting that I have to run to," he said suddenly. "You know, why don't you come with me?"

He began to gather his papers.

"You can come see what a meeting is like. It's going to be short because people are out of town, but they're going to serve lunch and I think you will definitely get something out of it."

"Um," I started.

"Come," he said, gesturing. "I'll tell them that you are a prospective joiner."

He stood up from the table.

"I mean, you will be one day."

3

There were twelve people split-up between two tables inside the high-ceilinged ballroom of the Chicago Plaza Hotel.

"Let's sit over at this one," said Marty, leading me to a table on the right side of the room.

Larry, the manager of a car dealership on Madison Street was there. So was Amy, who had some administrative title at the park district. Though everyone in the room except Marty and myself were wearing buttons with names and titles as big as a giant smiley face cookie on their chest (I think Marty decided not to wear it because I didn't have one), I noticed that Amy had large bold letters on hers that said, "Past President," from some year. You could just tell she loved being the past president from some year.

On the far end of the table, I met Matt, who was a vice president of a branch of some large bank, and Wayne, who was the current President of the Better Business Club of Greater Chicagoland and a stock advisor for J&L Investments. Wayne asked me about what college I was going to go to and then gave me a short sales pitch about how beneficial it would be for my future to join the Better Business Club of Greater Chicagoland. Finally, I met Rick and Dana, both from Titan Sports, a non-profit organization that helped run the park district ice sledding league for children with physical disabilities. There were several other men in a mix of suits and seasonal sweaters at the adjoining table that I had not personally met with, but I'm sure they thought they were very important in their own rights because I could see that each one of them had "Past something or another" in large bold letters on their giant pins.

"Time for tickets," said Marty, turning to me. "But you don't have to get any."

The tickets Marty was referring to were the weekly raffle tickets each member of the Club would buy. Red tickets were two dollars and blue tickets were one dollar. The winner of the red ticket raffle would get half of the total amount of the pot with the other half going to pay administrative expenses for the Better Business Club. The winner of the blue tickets would be entered into the end of the month raffle and would get some fractional percentage of the total amount remaining from each of the weeks. I think Larry had explained how they calculate the percentage for the blue ticket raffle, but I forgot it the moment he told me to tell you the truth.

Anyway, I felt obligated to buy the tickets because I was going to have lunch. At least I thought I should buy a red ticket for that week's raffle. Wayne greeted me at the raffle table with another firm handshake.

"You don't have to get any," he murmured, explaining the intricacies of the calculation of the blue ticket raffle, the same explanation that Larry had just given me, but not as concise.

"It's okay," I said after a short pause. "I'll get a red one."

"Okay, then," he said with a slight nod.

I pulled out my wallet and realized I only had a twenty dollar bill. I looked over at the table and saw twelve dollars in singles.

"I only have a twenty," I said, leaning forward confidentially.

"It's all right," he said, waving me off gently. "You don't have to buy one."

In an awkward silence, I casually slipped the bill back into my wallet and walked back to my seat next to Marty.

"Matt will lead us today in the pledge of allegiance," announced Wayne proudly from a podium draped in Better Business Club patches in the front of the room. Everyone stood up and put their hand over their heart.

"I pledge allegiance to the Flag of the United States of America. And to the Republic for which it stands, one nation, under God, indivisible, with liberty and justice for all," said everyone loudly in joined voices.

"Amen," said Wayne, swiveling around on his heels back to the podium. "Now, we will recite the Declaration of the Better Business Club of Greater Chicagoland." With every Better Business Club member still standing, Wayne turned back toward the flag and led the reciting. It went on for a couple of minutes, but my mind kind of drifted and I was watching everyone's lips silently flap for a few moments. Before we sat down, Wayne turned back around toward the podium and formally announced that there were a couple of "new faces" at the meeting today. A man named Phil from a new gas station on Orleans Street stood and said, "Hello," with a half-wave.

Then Marty introduced me.

"This is Cameron," said Marty, gesturing. "He is thinking about making the terrible mistake of starting a pre-law program at college next fall."

He smiled faintly. In fact, everyone kind of smiled faintly, and for some reason it reminded me of the time I had misspelled Albuquerque in my home room's fifth grade spelling competition, where I took second place to Sarah Lambert.

"He's a senior in high school, but be nice to him—he's working in an Honors Internship Program at the State's Attorney's Office this semester and you never know, he could *be* the State's Attorney or something one day," said Marty, smiling faintly again.

I bent forward and waved under gritted teeth.

As Wayne started announcing several upcoming events, a server named Tanya came around and passed out spinach salad. The spinach salad was drenched in a creamy garlic dressing. I listened to Wayne and ate the salad and looked across the room and listened to several conversations around me. As Marty started to whisper quietly in my ear about the Club and what they do as far as handing out grants, Tanya cleared the spinach salad plates from the tables and started to serve small bowls of chicken noodle soup.

It was wonderful soup. The layer of chicken grease floating above the white meat looked delicious.

When Wayne finished with his remarks, they held the raffles and you will just have to believe me when I tell you that Wayne won both the red and the blue contests. I'm not kidding. I'm not saying that Wayne fixed the red or the blue or both raffles, I'm just saying that I wasn't totally shocked when he had both winning numbers.

"Twelve bucks," said Matt, handing the small pile of largely singles to Wayne, who flashed a big grin. You should have seen how happy he was.

"This has never happened before, has it?" asked Wayne, clearly tickled with the feat.

As I stared into the excitement on his face, it started to look to me like it very well could have been the highlight of his week. I began to think that if I were to one day ever look happy enough after winning twelve bucks in a twelve-something person raffle I was presiding over as Wayne did that day that it would make someone think that it very well could have been the highlight of my week, I'd want someone to just shoot me.

This was the future Wayne said that I had to look forward to? I thought to myself.

I mean it really was depressing. All someone has to do is tell you how beneficial it would be for your future to join the Better Business Club of Greater Chicagoland and then five minutes later be excited as hell over winning twelve bucks in a twelve person raffle they were presiding over to be depressing. It wouldn't have been half as depressing, I don't think, if Wayne hadn't thrusted a clenched fist into the air like he had won the godforsaken jackpot at the State of Illinois Lottery.

The pasta primavera that was served for the main entrée was my cholesterol intake for the week. I really think that they thought that if they weren't going to get us with the spinach salad or the chicken noodle soup, they would get us with the creamy pasta primavera. I tore off a piece of the garlic bread from the side of my plate and there was so much butter on the bread that I could hardly taste the garlic.

Our table was pretty quiet at first, but then Amy asked me what type of law I wanted to study in college which led to a long back story about how she was once in pre-med and almost went to medical school.

"I see you were the past president of the Better Business Club of Greater Chicagoland," I said, pointing to her button and changing the subject. I think she blushed.

"Oh," she giggled. She giggled and giggled and giggled. "Well, that was a long time ago. But yes."

I looked over at Larry and he was slouched over, scooping the pasta business-like into his mouth while staring down at his plate. It was pretty quiet for awhile again. I think everyone was waiting for someone to start one of those stupid, neutral conversations that would involve the entire table. I mean the alternative was to slouch over your plate and scoop your pasta business-like like Larry.

"When's that marathon you're running in?" Rick asked Dana loudly.

Suddenly, we had our topic. Now everyone at the table just had to join in.

"Three weeks from Sunday," said Dana with extremely attentive eyes.

"What marathon is that?" asked Amy a little too enthusiastically.

"The Miami Marathon," said Dana in a rising voice.

"Wow," said Amy, raising her eyebrows.

"Did you ever run in the Chicago Marathon?" I asked Dana.

"Yeah," she said, laughing. "I fell face down in that one."

"Don't they close Lakeshore for it?" asked Marty, leaning forward.

"Well, they do it on the inner drive," said Dana, gesturing. "It starts at Grant Park and it goes all the way down to Addison and then back."

"Wow," said Amy, raising her eyebrows again.

Wayne excused himself after having finished off the pasta primavera and started talking with someone at the other table. Larry was still slouched over his plate eating. So was Matt.

"There are a lot of people out there usually?" asked Rick, lightly tapping the tips of his fingers together.

"Yeah," said Dana. "The Chicago Marathon is getting pretty big. They actually had to move it back a couple of weeks this year because of the Bears game."

"I'm sure that traffic at Soldier Field was more than the usual terrible if they closed down the streets around there for the marathon," said Marty as he drew his glass to his mouth and sipped his water.

"At least they don't have to worry about the Cubs playing in October," I said in a voice dropping into a sarcastic tone.

"Could you imagine?" said Marty, setting his glass on the table. "Could you imagine having to close down Addison Street for the marathon on a day of a Cubs playoff game?"

Everyone seemed to ponder that thought for a moment because the table got very quiet suddenly.

"When I first started running in it three years ago, the Cubs did have a playoff game on the same day, but they were in Atlanta," said Dana as she settled back in her chair.

Wayne was back at the podium and announced that Rick and Dana had a video presentation about the park district ice sledding league for children with physical disabilities and he announced it in such a fantastic way you would think a hundred and fifty people were packed in an auditorium instead of the twelve of us sitting and eating pasta primavera.

At first, the video presentation had a few technical glitches when the laptop Rick brought couldn't play the clip he had selected.

"Ice sledding at midnight," said Marty humorously as he pointed to the black screen on the wall. Larry laughed at that remark. So did Matt. Phil, who was stretching his legs at the other table, got a kick out of that one too. He laughed with a gorgeous mouth full of pasta.

"We did a run through this morning because I was afraid of this happening," said Dana, looking slightly flushed.

"Two of them," added Rick excitedly.

As I looked around the room, the primavera sat heavily in my stomach. While we waited for the video to start playing, Tanya picked up our finished plates and served dessert. The chilled scoop of vanilla ice cream sitting in front of me had a thick strawberry stripe drizzled on top. I thought about how it was somebody's job to drizzle that strawberry stripe on the ice cream knowing it was going to be eaten by the twelve of us. I thought about how I would hate a job like that. I mean, if I were going to be a strawberry striper, I would want the Queen of England to eat it.

Everyone started eating the ice cream right away except for Matt, who was too busy shoving the remaining pasta primavera into a Styrofoam container Tanya had handed him. I pictured Matt opening that container in his office at the bank for an afternoon snack and then I looked down at the globs of grease pooled on the side of my plate. I guess you can't complain about free food though.

The flickering on the screen turned into a full picture. Soon, there was audio to go along with it. The ice sledding league was designed for children between the ages of six and twelve with physical disabilities. There was an eight-year-old boy, whose leg had been amputated, being pushed in a sled around an ice rink, laughing.

"It's so much fun to be out on the ice," he said, flashing a wide smile. "I never thought I would be able to do something like that."

At the end of the video, Rick and Dana talked about volunteering time or donating old hockey equipment to the park district for the league.

"We have seasonal drop off boxes at City Hall and the ice rink at Millennium Park," said Rick, his eyes roving gradually around the ballroom.

"Even if you do the smallest thing, you can make a difference with these kids," said Dana, slightly nodding.

4

Splintering through the bunching grayness of the sky, the sun shined down and birds overhead flew south. I stood out in the frigid air on the pavement near the curb of the street and as I thanked Marty for lunch, the familiarity of a father-like presence abounded and I started to think about my father. I don't know why it kind of all of a sudden sprung on me. Maybe it was just being around Marty again and knowing how close the two of them used to be.

We parted ways under a tightening of coat collars and a promise I would tell my mother he said "Hello." As I crossed the street and looked back into the sky at the birds, I started to think about my father again and for some reason I began to drift into thought about the Cormorant Fishermen that he had told me about in Guilin on his trip to Guangxi, China. He would talk about how they would drift along the Li River in a small bamboo raft and use the cormorants to dive under the water and catch the fish. I remembered how he said the fishermen would bring the cormorants back to the boat by the ropes around their bodies and how each one would have five or six fish in its throat, but couldn't swallow them because of a ring fastened around its neck.

"Cameron, it's my job, goddamn it, to teach you how to fish in life," he would often tell me in his serious voice, parlaying it to my life.

It was only after the stock market had crashed in the wake of the financial meltdown and he had killed himself that I remembered him telling me in the weeks leading up to the incident, as if coming from the lips of a broken man, "I want you to know that you have learned from me over the last sixteen years, not one hundred percent, but a lot, and you should know that I felt it was my duty to put you on a path so that you could make a living and I feel I've taught you how to fish and now you have to pick it up from here."

Why did he jump from a stool with a rope tied around his neck in the basement of the house? This is something I have repeatedly asked myself. They found him with his legs dragging on the floor, which meant that he had to have bent his legs when he jumped to keep them from touching.

When I think of my father's death, I think of three things. I think first of the actor F. Murray Abraham as Antonio Salieri in the movie *Amadeus* when he was on the floor in the beginning and he had just slashed his wrists and the violins of Symphony No. 25 in G Minor start in. It's the violins starting in that I think of the most. Secondly, I think about the Chinese Twenty Yuan Bill with the picture of the Li River and the Karst Peaks near Guilin he brought back for me as a present from his trip to Guangxi. Finally, I think about the day of the funeral. I remember standing in my overcoat and dark suit during the funeral tugging nervously at my tie, feeling the cold gray air rushing my cheeks while looking at the hole in the ground, thinking about the desperate violence that must have occurred when he had jumped.

Lately, I have found myself wondering what he possibly could have been thinking about just before he jumped. Standing on the stool on the edge of life between the past and the future with the thick leather belt noosed around his neck after having lost almost everything—maybe he was just hoping to God it wasn't going to be an unsuccessful attempt and wake up one day from a coma in a hospital with a bedpan and a feeding tube, finding himself with a brain injury of some sort that he had suffered due to the lack of oxygen he received because of the tight knot of the noose. I regret that I obsess over things like this, but I just can't help it sometimes.

At the intersection up the block, I decided to call my friend Eric to see if he had any old hockey equipment to donate to the park district for the kids from the video. Eric is one of those people that never throws anything out. I dialed his number on my cell phone and waited on the curb while it started ringing.

"Hey," said Eric with light chatter in the background.

"Listen, do you have any old hockey equipment you can part with?" I asked curiously.

"Ah, probably," he answered.

"Good," I said excitedly. "I need it. I just saw a presentation about this non-profit organization that donates old hockey equipment to the park district for kids with physical disabilities."

I shaded the sun from my eyes.

"What are you doing today?" I asked after a slight pause.

"Believe it or not, I'm dressed up as Santa Claus as we speak," he said.

"You are?" I asked.

"Yes," he said. "It might sound ridiculous, but yesterday this guy at work came in and asked me if I would like to dress up as Santa Claus today for these second and third graders from Cabrini at the holiday festival at Daley Plaza."

"Does he know you're Jewish?" I asked casually.

"I don't know if he knows that I'm Jewish," he said, laughing humorously. "I don't think it really matters. Do I have to be Catholic to dress up as Santa Claus for some kids?"

"I think it's all right," I said.

"I actually told him he should talk to Brian," he said after a slight hesitation. "You know, Brian Preston. I was like, 'He'd be the perfect Santa Claus.' And so it's a long story because, you know, he's a little portly and, well, he took a little offense to it. He's like, 'Thanks for throwing me under the bus.'"

He cleared his throat.

"That guy Dan you met at that game that one time, the one who works with me, he heard our conversation," he said. "He was like, 'I'll do it. I'll be Santa.'"

He cleared his throat again.

"But I'd be Santa over Dan," he insisted. "Dan doesn't look like Santa Claus. He's too thin. He'd probably drop an f-bomb or something around the kids anyway."

"Where are you?" I asked. "Are you at work?"

"I'm actually on the train," he said. "I'm dog sitting for my brother and sister-in-law this week and I think I left my beard on my brother's kitchen counter, so, I am heading over there for a second to pick it up."

There was a short pause.

"I actually think he might have some old skates," he added.

"Great," I said. "You want to meet me at Johnnie's Grille in, say, forty-five minutes before heading to the festival?"

"Um, sure," he said, his words trailing off.

5

A train passed overhead on Wells Street powdering the old snow dust into the air with the new. I followed the herd of hats down the street and the falling swirls of snow. Smoke from the woman's mouth next to me carried on a muted conversation with the smoke from the woman's mouth on the other side of her. As I passed an ice cream shop on the corner of the street on the way to the bus stop, I started to think about the previous Sunday and the conversation Chloe and I had at dinner.

"Chloe, where does ice cream come from?" I had asked, just wondering what a four-year-old might say.

"The ice cream store," she said.

"Yes," I said. "And where does the ice cream store get the ice cream?"

"From God," she said. "Yes, from God," she re-affirmed.

"That sounds like some ice cream store," I said. "You'll have to ask your daddy about that."

"Daddy!" Chloe yelled as she raced into the kitchen. "Uncle Cameron asked me where ice cream came from and I told him the ice cream store," she said, recounting our conversation. "And then he asked where the ice cream store got the ice cream and I said, um, God."

"Yes, Chloe, the ice cream store gets its ice cream from God," he said, gently. "The ice cream maker gets the milk from cows and from the land and turns it into ice cream."

The bus heading north pulled up to the curb splattering snow around its tires. I sat toward the center of the bus among a crowd looking out the window at the passing landscapes. The blur of hoods and hats on the street offered faces I would never see and lives I would never know. My phone started to vibrate. It was a number I didn't recognize. I let it go to voicemail and then listened to the message. It was my cousin's husband David Adelman. David was a Financial Advisor and he had recently switched jobs. I had heard from my mom that he was going to try to approach me for a meeting.

"This is my favorite seat on the bus," said a tall, slender man sitting down in the seat across from me. "I love the center."

"Yeah," I said in a sarcastic tone. "Watch your knees as people pass."

Just as I said it, a man walked by brushing the tops of our knees with his briefcase. I turned away, looking out the window.

"What did you say your name was?" the man asked suddenly.

"What?" I asked, surprised because I had not told him my name.

"What did you say your name was?" the man asked again.

"Ah, Cameron," I said, finally.

"Cameron, I'm Miguel," said the man, leaning forward with intense eyes. "Cameron, have you thought about Jesus Christ?"

I looked at him without saying anything.

"I've been saved by Christ and I'm going to Spain out of his goodwill and getting away from this cold for awhile and away from all my contacts to spread the word about Jesus."

"I don't really care to discuss it," I said after a slight hesitation.

"Cameron, have you ever been to Zoo Lights before?" asked Miguel.

"Um—," I started.

"They have Christmas lights in patterns," Miguel explained. "Little displays throughout the zoo in Lincoln Park by the cages."

"I haven't," I said, shaking my head side to side.

"It's really nice," Miguel began again. "You walk around with cider and it's free. Not the cider, but the admission. You should go sometime."

I nodded absently.

"Do you like tapas, Cameron? Have you been to a tapas bar before?"

"Yeah, tapas bars are fun," I said, gradually looking away.

"There's a good tapas bar right up here on La Salle," said Miguel.

"Yeah, Café Ramblas," I said. "I've been there."

"Have you been to that Brazilian Steakhouse on LaSalle?" he asked, pointing out the window to the restaurant on the corner of the street.

"Listen," I broke in. "I want to get your thoughts on something."

"Sure, Cameron," said Miguel, his pupils widening.

"Do you think it's all right for someone who isn't Christian to dress up like Santa Claus?" I asked.

"Does he believe in Christ?" he asked, his voice rising.

"Well, he's Jewish," I said. "He was asked by someone at work to dress up as Santa for second and third graders and believe me he's doing it for the kids. But this guy, he does a lot of things for kids. For example, he's going to give me some old hockey equipment to donate to a group of kids with physical disabilities. Now, he's not Mother Theresa by any means, I don't want you thinking that, but he's a great guy and he means well."

"You know what, Cameron?" asked Miguel eagerly. "You should ask that question to Father Reilly. You should come with me to see Father Reilly this afternoon. I think he would have some interesting thoughts on that."

"You know, I would love to meet Father Reilly, but I can't this afternoon," I said, shaking my head.

As I sat there, I tried to think of any reason why I couldn't go.

"You see, I have this Better Business of Chicagoland meeting," I said, finally. "I have to be there. I'm presiding over the ticket raffle. There's actually two raffles; a blue and a red one. The winner of the red ticket raffle gets half of the total amount of the pot with the other half going to pay administrative expenses for the Club. The winner of the blue ticket one is entered into the end of the month raffle and gets some fractional percentage of the total amount remaining from each of the weeks. I would sit here and explain how the percentage for the blue ticket raffle is calculated, but it's very complex."

6

The large colorful banner on the wall by the door advertising the spicy fries at Johnnie's Grille as "Famous" was almost mesmerizing if you stared at it for awhile. I took a couple of spicy fries from the grease-stained carton in front of me as I stared at the depth of the black in the letter "F" of the word Famous. In the silence of the hum of the heater, Eric, dressed in his Santa Claus suit, approached with a small white shopping bag in one hand and his beard in the other.

"Hey," I said, flashing a smile.

"It's official," said Eric. "This suit rocks."

He laughed loudly.

"I just met this girl on the train I normally never would have said anything to," he said, laughing humorously again.

He leaned forward.

"Here," he said, handing me a shopping bag of old hockey equipment. "Sorry, it took longer than I thought."

"Thanks," I said, holding the handle of the bag. "No problem."

I looked at his Santa's beard as he turned it over in his hands.

"The dog was chewing on it," he said. "I walked in and the beard was on the floor and it was in his mouth. Is it very noticeable?"

"Its fine," I said, trying to be reassuring.

I sat back in my chair, placing the shopping bag under the table near my feet. Eric sat down in the chair across from me.

"Where does your brother and sister-in-law live?" I asked, turning toward him.

"Andersonville," he said, momentarily still distracted with the beard.

"Where did they go?" I asked. "On a trip?"

"They went to North Carolina to visit her family," he said, straightening slightly.

He looked back down at the beard as if to inspect it again.

"How's your brother's place?" I asked.

"They have a nice place," he said.

"And the dog?" I asked. "Like what do you do? Lie around petting the dog all day while watching T.V.?"

"Pretty much," he said.

As a short silence ensued, he looked down at his watch.

"I should probably go," he said suddenly. "I don't want to be late."

He stood up from the table with his beard spread in his hands as if he was once again inspecting it.

7

The blots of a light snowfall sprinkled a crowd of skaters dotting the perimeter of the ice rink at Millennium Park. I dropped off the bag of old hockey equipment at the drop off box and then stood idly at the edge of the ice rink listening to the snow fall while watching the skaters take a couple of turns around the ice.

Just for something to do, I walked up the snowy concrete steps leading up to the band shell. An orchestra was playing an old Christmas song to a scattered crowd gathering across the snow covered lawn beneath the crisscrossing steel sound system stretching above.

"Oh, there it is," said a woman in a ski jacket to her friend, lifting her oversized dark sunglasses to get a better look at Cloud Gate.

As I looked over, there were people gathered around its base producing countless reflections in its fun house-like mirrors.

I walked through the 2.5 acre Lurie Gardens in the southeast corner of the park. As I stared at the snow tipped gardens, I noticed there was a steel frame around the tall Evergreen and Deaduous trees. A sign said that in "…7-10 years, the trees will fill the frame, creating the appearance of a solid green hedge."

There were benches bordering the sculpted hedges throughout the garden, some six planks wide, others twelve. A wooden pedestrian footbridge was suspended over an empty crevice where shallow water would pool in the summer.

"Everything is either square or symmetrical," a woman in passing said, pointing about the garden with a watchful eye.

Flanking the crevice was a rustic white stone wall, smooth and steep on one side, rough on top. A pebble pathway lined by smooth white stone led from one garden to the next while a groundskeeper continually swept the stray pebbles from the pedestrian footbridge. As the wind swung in off the lake, I decided to go warm up inside the Art Institute.

Each step up the Michigan Avenue entrance front steps was like a frosted cupcake of snowflakes and sprinkled salt. The two bronze lions flanking the steps were given a new white coat of snow armor. I looked at the north lion and thought of Dolan. "In like a lion…"

A crowd of children on a school field trip were at the door. As I walked past them into the front hall, overlapping echoes bounced off paintings and walls, mixing soft voices with loud into a raised buoyant pitch of chatter. The teacher leading the children was discussing with one of the other teachers whether it was more important to see the Collection of Arms and Armor or the Thorne Miniature Rooms. I stood by the blowing air of the vent and warmed myself as I listened to them discussing it. After some indecision, they decided on the Miniature Rooms.

After a few moments I was warm and I walked past the children and up the stairs to the galleries.

"Cameron!" someone shouted.

I looked over and saw a familiar face. It was Todd Barrett. Todd had made All-Conference in football last year from Armitage High and was now a freshman at Missouri.

"Barrett," I said. "Todd Barrett! How the hell are you? What are you doing here?"

"I'm meeting my parents for lunch," he said. "I'm on break. You?"

"I actually just came in to roam and warm-up," I said, gesturing.

"Crazy son of a bitch," he said, pointing at the van Gogh Self-Portrait on the wall in front of me.

"Yeah," I said, staring at the painting.

I turned toward him.

"How's football?"

"I quit," he said in a short sigh.

"What?" I asked a bit unevenly.

"I quit," he said again, looking flushed.

I stared at him almost unbelieving.

"No, it's the truth," he continued. "I told my dad I was never going to have another grown man yell at me ever again."

I stood there, listening.

"It was just—well," he started again, "one morning, the position coach, he was yelling, 'Not fast enough! Not fast enough!' and under my breath I was like, 'Go fuck yourself.'"

He paused for breath.

"I mean, it was six in the morning, none of us were playing, we were all red-shirted, we were all exhausted, the team was doing terrible, we only had like 3 or 4 wins, we were not going to a Bowl game," he said, leaning forward."I was like, 'This sucks!'"

He hesitated.

"So I quit the team," he said flatly. "It is the best decision I have ever made."

He rubbed his forehead.

"I don't know, Cameron, you'll see, college is different," he said. "Nobody cares about your records in high school."

He stared at the van Gogh Self-Portrait as if he was in a faraway place.

"You know, I kind of miss high school," he said in a voice that dropped into a sentimental tone.

He looked at me closely.

"I miss winning conference last year, you know?" he said. "I miss the confidence of being good at something."

It was how sentimental he was becoming that started to make it depressing. I quickly started to think of a way to escape.

"You know what?" I said, looking down at my watch. "I almost forgot. I gotta go see Father Reilly."

It was the only thing that occurred to me.

"Father who?" he asked.

"Yeah, Father Reilly," I said. "I'm actually already late. I've been saved by Jesus Christ, recently that is, and I'm going to Spain out of his goodwill and getting away from this cold for awhile to spread his word."

"Spain?" he said confusedly.

"Yeah," I said, looking down at my watch. "Oh, I probably should go. I don't want to be late."

I looked at my watch again, but this time more dramatically.

"Yeah, I'm really late," I said. "You know, for Father Reilly."

As I walked down the stairs, I pretended to leave, but then quickly ducked down the back stairs into a gallery of photographs. There were rows and rows of framed photographs hung along the walls leading from one room to the next. Encased in glass on one of the walls was a portrait of ex-slave Frederick Douglass from 1847. I looked closely at his clothes and his expression, and the way he held his body. His hair was parted, neatly combed to the right without one hair out of place. His eyebrows were arched with a wrinkle in his mid-forehead. He was standing stiffly and was wearing a dark suit, a leaf patterned vest, and a white shirt and tie. As I looked into his eyes, it was as if he was looking through me.

How does he want to be remembered? I asked myself, wiping sweat from my forehead with the back of my hand.

I studied the portrait. It was a modern affirmation of existence, the epitome of an intellectual "Kilroy was here!" As I looked closely again at his eyes, I realized that I wasn't exactly sure if I, myself, knew how I wanted to be remembered.

On another wall, there was an 1891 portrait by Kathe Kollwitz of a young boy sitting, dressed in a formal dress jacket with slicked back hair. With his right arm bent, the back of his hand creased his cheek carrying the weight of his head. He looked off center, and there was depth to his eyes. He looked as if he was bored sitting there, but he was telling me through his eyes, as if repressed, that he was a boy that had dreams, but didn't know how to reach them or if he would ever have a chance to achieve them. As I stared at him, the portrait looked unfinished. I asked myself why Kollwitz didn't include a background. Perhaps, I mustered, because he had a lot of living to do.

Kollwitz was waiting for life to fill it in, I thought to myself.

As I stood there thinking about the background of the Kollwitz portrait of the boy and the photograph of Frederick Douglass, I found myself oddly short of breath.

What is the matter with me? I thought to myself.

As I wiped the sweat from my forehead, I caught a glimpse of the shadow of my face in the metal frame of a 1920 self-portrait of Archibald J. Motley, Jr., a young African-American male who had attended the School of the Art Institute, and I looked very pale. I felt my head to see if I had a fever. I started to think about how sentimental Todd Barrett got about high school and then I started to think about my father. It started to feel stuffy and as I took a couple deep breaths, my shirt started to cling to my back in dampness. As I began to feel light-headed, I unzipped my coat in a cold sweat.

8

Outside the Art Institute, I rushed down the whitened steps
and past the lions. As the cold wind blew hard through the air, I
zipped my coat back up and tightened its collar. I was breathing in
gasps and it was only then I fully realized that I had been thinking
about how it was one year, to the day, that my father had killed
himself right before the cold sweat came on.

I started to walk up the street thinking back about my father
and then I started to think about the person who had to drizzle the
strawberry stripe on the ice cream at the Better Business Club of

Chicagoland's luncheon. That person had to drizzle the strawberry stripe so perfectly knowing it was just going to be eaten by the twelve of us because everyone else was out of town. This is what I was thinking. I wondered if that person ever thought how he was going to be remembered and whether he thought of himself in the context of being the person who drizzled the strawberry stripe.

As I was thinking about that I saw a man across the street dressed up as a giant Chocolate Peanut Butter Cup handing out samples of candy to people. I stood there for a moment watching and I started to think to myself whether it was better to be remembered as the person whose job it was to drizzle a strawberry stripe on ice cream for the twelve of us at the Better Business Club luncheon or to be known as the person who dressed up as a giant Chocolate Peanut Butter Cup handing out samples of candy to people like the guy on the street.

Either one was probably better than having to be the woman sitting on the horse carriage at the corner looking bored as hell while waiting for riders. That woman looked so bored. Her head was resting on a bent arm, not unlike the boy in the Kollwitz portrait, and she was leaning forward against the foot rest of the carriage. With all the snow it really looked like a pretty slow day for carriage riders, in all honesty. I would bet a lot of her day was spent in just that exact position. Maybe most of it. Maybe most days. I started to think about how she had to sit up there like Little Miss Muffet and wait for someone who wanted to be given a horse carriage ride through the midday traffic on a Thursday and how until she found that someone she had to smell that stinking horse's ass that looked to be just inches from her face.

I stood and watched the guy in the giant Chocolate Peanut Butter Cup costume wave to everyone who walked past him. To me, I don't know, he had this maniacal grin that was sewn into his costume and he looked so excited when these children walked past him that it reminded me of a child molester. I mean, he also had this gigantic tongue sewn into the costume and I thought the children probably thought he was cute with his oversized orange shoes, but he looked like what a child molester would look like if I had ever seen one.

Anyway, I don't know if any of those jobs were better than the fake fashion photo shoot up the street that was trying to draw attention to a new French hairstyling mousse. As I stood there and watched, two models in ski jackets strutted back and forth on a small red carpet as a photographer in a camel coat snapped pictures. I buttoned my coat around my neck tightly and I started to wonder what was worse; the photographer pretending to take the pictures or the models walking back and forth aimlessly on the small red carpet. They were attracting some attention, though. I saw the guy in the giant Chocolate Peanut Butter Cup costume watching them. So was the woman that was bored to hell sitting in the horse carriage smelling the horse's ass.

To tell you the truth, I really felt bad for the guy who had to roll up the red carpet when they finished with the fake shoot. That would have to be one of the most depressing jobs. I mean, he was wearing a blazer over a wool sweater and everything. Did anyone tell him he was just going to be rolling up the carpet? It really didn't seem necessary. I pictured him getting ready in the morning and deciding to wear a wool sweater and a blazer knowing that he was going to just roll up the red carpet in a fake fashion photo shoot. I started to think about how I would hate to one day be on my deathbed and know that's what I did with my life.

It was cold and my cheeks were getting red and my shirt was still slightly damp from the cold sweat earlier, so, before I could catch pneumonia I walked into Macy's on State Street. Inside there were signs advertising huge sales everywhere. I rode the escalator up looking at all of the Christmas decorations feeling like the half-eaten fish in *The Old Man and the Sea*, not Santiago, but the fish. There was an old man with gray bushy hair playing *Don't Cry For Me, Argentina* from *Evita* on a Steinway grand piano near a bunch of leather couches on the third floor. There were four other men varying in ages sitting on the couches with shopping bags at their feet—all of them sitting quietly and waiting for someone else.

I took out *Tropic of Cancer* from my inner coat pocket and read a little. I always liked when Miller said "By morning something will happen" toward the end of the first chapter. People are always waiting for something to happen. As I sat back against the couch, I watched the old man play the piano for awhile under the small clatter by the escalators in the lobby. He was now playing *Memories* from *Cats*. He was closing his eyes as he played. I sat there and watched. His eyes were closed the entire time as he played. I can tell he was into the music. He was either into the music or far from it. As I sat there watching to see if he was going to open his eyes, I started to wonder whether my father ever asked himself how he wanted to be remembered one day. I wasn't sure. I didn't think he ever did. I think he was too busy having a nervous breakdown.

As I sat there, I thought about how there was so much I didn't understand about myself. In an attempt to sort it out, I started to think of several attributes that I would want to use to describe myself. I took out a pen and a small cocktail napkin I had taken from the Better Business Club luncheon. It had this beautiful grease splotch from the primavera on the side with the insignia from the hotel that seemed to soak through to the other side. Around the splotch I put the tip of the pen on the napkin and waited. As I waited, my phone started to vibrate. It was a text message from Darren, my partner on the debate team at school.

"You finish the argument for debate yet?" it said.

You probably should know that I had decided that I was going to quit the debate team at the end of the semester, but I hadn't told anyone yet. I don't know why, but it had started to feel increasingly meaningless. They were all little Dolans so full of themselves it would make you sick. They loved pissing on each other. God, did they love pissing on each other. And the coach. Judge Pinegrove. You should have seen the way he yelled at us.

"Like Caesar crossing the Rubicon!" That was his line to us.

He said that was what we should be thinking about when we stepped in front of the judges at every debate tournament. He would say it with clenched teeth and a Shakespearean tone and he would have the look of Almighty God in his eyes.

As I sat there staring at the text message waiting for something to happen, my mind started to drift. I began to think back about the Benjamin Banks Trial from earlier in the semester. I had not seen Henry Russell since the trial, but I could still picture the disappointment on his face. I imagined he just went home and cried after the jury read the verdict. I would think he cried alone because he was a widower and Susan, his daughter, had been murdered, and she was his only child and there was no one else I could think of. Like it always did, the thought of him crying alone made me sad as hell. To Russell, I wasn't someone that was just part of a ten week Illinois State High School Leaders Internship Program. I was as responsible for the not guilty verdict as the others. I am slow to remember what exactly it was that actually made me go that day to see him, but I remember it wasn't until I had left the third floor and the leather couches and the grand piano and was almost at Russell's door that I admitted to myself that it wasn't such a good idea.

9

"Just a minute," yelled a strained and muffled voice through the door. I stood on the front porch with my arms at my sides.

"Who is it?" asked the voice, clearly of an old man with bad hearing that was not expecting anybody.

"Mr. Russell, it's Cameron Hoffenberg with the State's Attorney's Office," I yelled.

"Hoffenberg?" he repeated.

I heard the steel bolt unlock as the door slowly opened. The outline of a darkened figure with poor posture came forward from the shadows.

"Hi, Mr. Russell," I said with a friendly wave.

He looked like death. He leaned toward me, squinting.

"Mr. Russell, can we talk for a few minutes?" I asked.

"I wasn't expecting to see you here," he said. "Did you find her?"

"No, Mr. Russell," I said. "I'm here because I just want to talk. Do you have a couple of minutes?"

After hesitating, he nodded, slowly backing away from the door.

I stepped into his apartment and whenever I step into a strange apartment that is on the creepy side I think of Jodie Foster walking into the serial killer's house in *Silence of the Lambs*. It was creepy because a lonely old man lived in it alone and it was the kind of dreary place you would imagine it would look like.

It seemed almost hardly lived in. In fact, it seemed empty and airless. That's probably a better description than creepy. It was gray and there were hardly any pictures on the walls. Seeing the bare walls made me sad as hell to tell you the truth. I told him how much I liked his apartment anyway. He nodded.

We walked through the foyer over to the living room. The floors were made of an old oak and it creaked with every step. I sat down on a reupholstered linen couch after Russell quickly dusted it with the back of his hand.

"Don't mind the balls of socks," said Russell, referring to several balls of socks lying on the floor. "The kitties like them."

I bent forward, nodding.

Just as he said that, I noticed that there was an overwhelming smell of cat liter filling the living room. It actually smelled like cat litter in the foyer too, but the smell was overwhelming in the living room. As I looked around, I knew how bad things had been over the last year. The place looked a little disheveled. Russell looked a little disheveled. Russell looked a lot disheveled. He had grown a pair of scraggly pork chop sideburns since the last time I had seen him.

"You're lucky you caught me when you did," he said. "I was just about to go for my afternoon walk. If you came five minutes later, I would have been gone."

"Where do you usually go on your walk?" I asked.

"Well, that depends," he said. "If it's Tuesday, you see, then I walk down Addison to the lakefront and then I walk over to Belmont Harbor and back."

There was a pause.

"But today's not Tuesday," he said. "Today is Thursday. So, today, I will walk over to Clark Street and down to Belmont and then take Belmont to Broadway over to Addison."

"Oh," I said.

"I usually do that twice, you see, and then I stop off at that grocery store on Broadway and Addison and pick-up dinner for my kitties," he said.

I nodded with a lot of enthusiasm. My nose was starting to twitch because of the smell of the cats in there. To tell you the truth, I was afraid I was going to get a nosebleed. I mean the cat litter was so strong in the living room it almost completely masked the old moth ball-like smell I had initially smelled in the foyer.

"That's a good walk," I said.

"Yeah, well, I can usually only do it from March to the early or middle part of December depending on when it snows and then I strictly get my exercise by walking to that grocery store—the one on Broadway and Addison I was telling you about—I strictly walk to and from that grocery store there when its snowing," he said.

He made a small gesture with his hands.

"Susie used to come visit twice a week and sometimes it would be on Thursday and she would go with me on the walk," he said.

I nodded knowing that living alone as old as Russell was scared the hell out of me. I looked over at the bookcase against the wall and I noticed a black and white picture of a young Russell in an army uniform smiling and another man in an army uniform standing beside him with the word "Bushmasters" written in the corner.

"I didn't know you were in the Bushmasters," I said.

He turned, looking over his shoulder at the bookcase.

"Company B, 1st Battalion, 158th Regiment Combat Team," he said, pointing up at the picture. "That man—the man in the picture with me—he was a buddy of mine."

I looked closely at the other man. He looked like someone who was around my age at the time or maybe a little older. He had this very easy smile on his face.

"He died on the island of New Guinea," he said. "Lieutenant James Abernathy. That was over fifty years ago. Fifty years—fifty years! Can you believe it?"

I shook my head.

"You know, I don't think I've said his name out loud in maybe ten years," he said. "You see, I was eighteen when they shipped me out to the Philippines. Eighteen. You can imagine the impact it has had on my life all these years."

He settled his thoughts.

"Fifty years," he began again. "I remember Abernathy was from a small town in Iowa. We met in boot camp. We trained in the Panama. But the Japs—the Japs were fierce."

There was a short silence.

"Some of the Jap camps we overpowered," he started, "we saw they ate fish heads and rice."

He looked at me squarely.

"Once you were there for awhile and saw what you were up against, you got mean," he said. "They shot medics. They shot a lot of medics. When they said we were helping them die for the Emperor, they meant it. They were not going to give up."

I sat there attentively.

"The Japanese were a master of camouflage," he said. "They would hide in the jungle, hide in trees."

He took a long breath.

"They would hide in the coconut trees," he said. "We would spray the trees with M-16 machine guns and sometimes they would tie themselves in the trees so they wouldn't even fall out."

"How did Lieutenant Abernathy die?" I asked.

"Well, we lost six out of twelve men in our platoon in two nights," he said, staring at me with a death stare. "Six of twelve if you could imagine. One shell came over and killed three guys in the hole next to me. He was one of them."

I sat back against the couch in thought and then looked back over at the bookcase against the wall and noticed an old picture of Russell with his wife and Susan. It had a layer of dust on its plastic frame, but it had fresh fingerprint smudges as if it had been recently held. They were smiling these great big smiles that went from ear-to-ear. They looked so happy. I couldn't stand it. I couldn't stand any of it. I couldn't stand that Russell's wife had died of lung cancer and wasn't there anymore to breathe some color into the dreary apartment and some life into Russell himself. I couldn't stand the smile on Lieutenant Abernathy's face knowing the picture was probably taken weeks before he died from the shell in the foxhole. I couldn't stand the scraggly pork chop side burns

Russell had grown or the fact that you couldn't even smell the old moth ball-like smell anymore in the foyer because of the cat litter.

It made me depressed as hell to think about how Susan would come on Thursdays to walk with him and how he now would have to walk alone. I felt so sorry for him. He seemed like a lost soul, caught in the cracks of society in a different world. I started to recall the words of my father: "It's my job to teach you how to fish."

It's

I pictured the ease in which my father stepped onto the old creaky stool, wanting out of his own body, his own skin. It was the stool I used to sit in at my desk at home to do homework after school. I thought about the cold darkness he must have felt standing barefoot on the stool, one step away and all around him no safe steps. He couldn't wear shoes. He would have been too tall with his shoes.

my job

A life of hard work with nothing to show for it. In his mind,
he was his greatest fear, Willy Loman from *Death of a Salesman*.
And he knew it. He lost much more than just his livelihood. He
lost his manhood, his sense of self, anything that he could identify
with and he struggled with the very essence of living with who he
had become. He had been looking forward to that day for some
time I imagined. He probably jumped immediately. No second
thoughts.

to teach you

Tying the thick leather belt around the wide steel pipe in the
cobwebby ceiling of the damp, dark basement, he must have been
desperate. I pictured him taking great care making the knot on the
buckle of the belt like the good fisherman he was. Looping it under
his chin, then over his head. Yanking it viciously tight with a slip
knot. One that wouldn't break loose when the pressure of his
weighty body came crashing down from the stool.

how to

I thought about how they found him slouched over, legs dragging on the floor, neck broken, dangling. I thought about how he had to have purposely lifted his knees up into the air as he dangled so that he wouldn't touch the floor.

fish

I sat there staring at an overflowing bowl of cat food and thought: Live alone like old man Russell with all his cats or go out knees bent as you dangle so that you don't touch the floor with your feet. This could not be how I would be remembered. It couldn't be. I needed to get out of there. I couldn't stand sitting there for one more minute.

"Mr. Russell, I am so sorry," I said, flushed, looking at my watch. "I totally forgot about the kids from Cabrini at the holiday festival at Daley Plaza. I actually have to go. I'm dressing up as Santa Claus this year for these second and third graders. They're bringing the kids there."

I stood up, the compulsive liar that I was.

"Well, I'm about to go on my walk," he said. "Do you want to go one time around with me if it's not snowing?"

"I'd love to, Mr. Russell, but you see, what I just realized is that I have to go pick up my beard," I said. "I'm dog sitting for my brother and sister-in-law this week because they're in North Carolina and I think I left my beard on my brother's kitchen counter so, you see, I have to head over there to pick it up."

As I rubbed my forehead, he stood there looking at me.

"Well, okay, just let me get my umbrella and I'll walk you out."

He paused a moment.

"Where's my list?" he asked himself, searching his pockets, and then the countertop in the kitchen. "Here it is," he said, grabbing it from the top of a pile of papers. It had two words written on it in large black capital letters: CAT FOOD.

"It's supposed to snow intermittently all afternoon," he said, picking up a long-necked umbrella.

He locked up the front door after petting two cats on their heads, though I think there may have been more because he yelled "good-bye" toward a blank wall in the empty foyer before shutting it. As we walked down the front stoop, it stopped snowing.

"Did you drive here?" he asked.

"No, I took the train," I said.

"Oh, I'll walk with you to Addison then," he said.

"Okay," I said.

We arrived at the Addison train stop and I told Russell that we would have a "rain check" on the walk for another time, but I think he thought I said something about rain outside because he lifted his umbrella in the air and looked up into the sky and said, "It's supposed to freeze up tonight." It wasn't his fault he was old and was a little hard of hearing. It was probably better that he didn't hear me anyway because I didn't want to give him false hope from the promise when I wasn't sure if I could actually come back and do it.

I watched him wave to me from the corner of the intersection and then walk down the street. I pictured Russell coming home after his walk to that empty, dreary apartment with food for his cats and it made me depressed as hell. When the train finally came, I'm sure Russell was somewhere down Clark Street heading toward Belmont on the first lap of his walk. I stepped into the half-empty train car and sat in an empty seat near the door obsessing about my future as a formal feeling of emptiness pitted itself deep in my stomach.

I glanced around the car and, to tell you the truth, I think I smelled like cats because I smelled cats. Unless the large plain woman taking up two seats in front of me was actually holding a cat in her lap, then I was the one who smelled like cats.

10

As I waited at the coffee shop for my cousin's husband,

David Adelman, to arrive, I watched people pass by on the street

with their formal faces and their formal coats and their formal

walks. For a moment, you would never know the economy was

having a meltdown by the way people frolicked in that five block

bubble of the Gold Coast. I started to think about Russell and about

the Russells of the world. The Russells and the Abernathy's. How

do the Dolans do it? How do the Dolans get to stand on the backs

of the Russells and the Abernathy's?

Across the street, the wind was blowing snow from one pile to another. As I sipped my coffee, I took out my primavera-stained napkin and waited for a word that I would use to describe myself. I thought about how I was waiting there for David to arrive and I wrote the word, *Good Cousin.*

I began to thumb through my past text messages on my phone and read an old one that Abigail had sent asking whether I wanted to help her pack later that day for her trip. I guess you could call Abigail my ex-girlfriend, but we were still kind of together. I know I haven't told you much about her. One thing I can tell you about her is that she is one of the biggest hypochondriacs that I have ever seen. For example, the previous year she had had her gallbladder out after complaining of a succession of stomachaches. Her mother had had her own gallbladder out a few years before, but it's normal for someone who is fifty-six years old and overweight or has gallstones to have their gallbladder removed.

I told Abigail that I thought she was just working herself up, you know, from the stress of grades and the A.C.T. and not knowing what college she was going to be going to. But she went to see some doctors. During one of her visits, her mother suggested removing her gallbladder. And the doctor was like, 'Well, we can do that.' It was one of those things that when you get it in your head you kind of convince yourself that it was it. I mean there is no reason a sixteen-year-old should get their gallbladder out just to have it out. Seriously, afterwards, she was the same.

You can't blame her though. Her younger sister Katie had died of a brain tumor a week before she turned 13. How can you blame someone for being a hypochondriac after something like that? Her sister's brain tumor was her gallbladder. In her mind it was. And when she had stomachaches, it was like her sister when she would complain about her headaches. Her parents had attributed her sister's headaches to stress at school, anxiety about her upcoming Bat Mitzvah, which was only weeks away, a sinus infection, even chlorine from their pool. They gave her aspirin.

They even took her in for a neural exam, but her motor skills were fine. The reason why her motor skills were fine was because the ping pong ball-sized tumor that they eventually found after rushing her to the hospital following a seizure at school was in the cerebellum, not the brain stem.

I'm sure that's what her mother was thinking when she suggested removing Abigail's gallbladder to the doctor. Can you imagine having to contemplate whether to donate your dead 13-year-old daughter's organs within moments of her dying? This is what Mrs. Fleming had to deal with. She told me about it once in a rare moment of candidness in the kitchen in their house before dinner one night. She told me she was indecisive, but that Abigail was adamant about it. The organs ultimately went to six people and saved six other lives and the funeral was held in the temple where the Bat Mitzvah was going to be. This is why I don't blame her.

I sipped my coffee and took out my wallet. I slid the Chinese Twenty Yuan Bill from its sleeve and stared at the picture of the Li River and Karst Peaks. After awhile, I noticed a homeless man walking around asking for change. There was a usual flow of homeless people that would come inside there because of the low rent hotel across the street. All the crazies stayed there. I remember the Cane Man's watery eyes, humbled by life, staring at you as you would walk into the coffee shop. Slouched over and propped up by his cane, he would ask you for your money on your way in and for your change on your way out.

There was Old Lady Lemon Fingers who would reach into the communal container of sliced lemons with her dirty fingers instead of using the spoon. One time, I watched her dig her entire fist into the rinds and touch all of the lemons. In all honesty, to this day, she is the reason why I won't take a lemon in my water. You never know if an Old Lady Lemon Fingers had been there.

There was a guy with cornrows that was mentally unsound and he would come grab your cup when you finished drinking and then fill it up with coffee and take it out to the street with him. I remember one day it was slow in there and only a few people were drinking coffee and he kept checking the garbage for a cup, talking gibberish to himself. He checked it nearly every five minutes. Another time, I saw him grab crusts of bread from someone's finished plate right off the table directly in front of me. A couple of times, I had made eye contact with him, but he was not the kind of person you would want to make eye contact with because he had wild eyes and he looked like he could snap at any minute. He actually wouldn't come into the coffee shop that often, but I would see him occasionally sleeping on the sidewalk outside the ATM vestibule of the Gold Coast Bank on Division Street.

Pillow Head was the kind of guy that would come into the coffee shop after rolling out of bed and his hair would be sticking straight up in an Alfalfa cowlick in the back, as if he had just rolled out of bed because he did just roll out of bed. I remember he would walk into the restaurant with torn khakis and yesterday's coffee stained cup in his hand and fill it up with the morning's coffee. To me, Pillow Head always looked like a guy that had worked in a pawn shop. I don't know why I thought that, but that's what I always thought when I looked at him.

And then there was the Crab Lady. The Crab Lady stood four feet and eleven inches tall and she had these high arching eyebrows and a scarf wrapped around her neck. She got the name Crab Lady because when she arched her eyebrows she really did look like a crab. The Crab Lady would always come into the coffee shop around five o'clock in the evening because that was the time they would giveaway leftover sandwiches from the afternoon. One day, I was sitting at a table near the windows and when the Crab Lady saw my gray sweatshirt with New York lettering, she started making anti-Semitic remarks. What a horrible woman she was.

I will tell you that I still think about the Crab Lady sometimes. I wonder about the Crab Lady, Cane Man, Old Lady Lemon Fingers, Cornrows, Pillow Head—the whole gang. I can't imagine where they are now. I tell myself not to think about them because it's too depressing, but sometimes I can't help it.

11

"I love it," said David after I asked him how he liked his new job. He was stuffed in the chair opposite me at the coffee shop. "I was born to do this. I really think I was. Things have been very busy. This economy has really been good for business."

"Oh, I'm sure," I said under a snap from the nearby fireplace.

"For the last couple months I haven't seen Julie," he said. "I come home at seven and you know, with kids, Julie's been with them all day and it's my turn to be with them and Julie goes off and gets her work done."

He drew a long breath.

"And she's had five parties the last couple of weeks so she's been really busy."

He hesitated.

"Anyway, I wanted to meet because I just want to talk. Not about the economy, but about life."

He leaned forward.

"I want you to know me in a different way—in a professional way outside the family stuff. It's really more for us to get to know each other better and to see if any of the services I have can help you in the future, as you go to college, and eventually enter the workforce, be in a better financial position."

He joined his hands together.

"Have you made a decision yet as to where you're going next fall?"

"Not yet."

"Have you started to think about what you want to study?"

"A little bit."

"Good. The key to a solid financial future is for you to eventually have streams of revenue regardless of your chosen profession. The key is to have vehicles of revenue-making—"

"Listen," I broke in, "I know we're talking about my future in strictly a financial context and with this economy I think about my financial future all the time, but, well, I saw this presentation on these kids with physical disabilities this afternoon. This one eight-year-old kid had his leg amputated and he was being pulled around in a sled and then I went to the Art Institute and I was looking at a self-portrait of Frederick Douglass."

"Frederick Douglass the ex-slave?" he asked.

"Yes! Frederick Douglass the ex-slave. It was from 1847 and I looked at the clothes he wore and the way he held his body and the way he parted his hair. There was not one hair out of place."

He nodded, unsure of where I was taking this.

"Not one. And his eyebrows were arched and he had this wrinkle in his mid-forehead. And his eyes. It was as if he was looking through you. I started to think about how it was a modern affirmation of existence, a graphic "Kilroy was here," which in turn made me think about how he wanted to be remembered. And then I saw the portrait of a young boy by Kathe Kollwitz from 1891. He was sitting, dressed in a formal dress jacket with slicked back hair. He was looking off center and he was telling me in his eyes that he had dreams but he didn't know if he was ever going to reach them. And as I stared at the picture I wondered why Kollwitz left the background unfinished and you know what I came up with?"

"I have no idea," said David. "What?"

"That Kollwitz left the background unfinished on purpose because the boy has a lot of living to do. Kollwitz was waiting for life to fill it in. And then I saw this guy in a Chocolate Peanut Butter Cup costume handing out candy on the street and this poor woman who was bored to death sitting in a carriage with her head close to the back of this horse that probably stunk and I thought about how she had to sit there until she found someone who wanted to take a carriage ride and it didn't seem too fair."

He sat there quietly, listening.

"And then there was this guy who rolled up a red carpet after a fake photo shoot. On the street, on Michigan Avenue, there was this guy whose job it was to get down on his hands and knees and roll up the red carpet and carry it up the street for the next fake shoot and he was wearing a blazer over a wool sweater and I started to think about how he woke up that morning knowing it was his job to roll up the red carpet when he chose to wear the blazer. And then I went to visit this old man whose daughter had been murdered. I had worked on the trial and he had these scraggly pork chop sideburns and about a thousand cats and he was a widower and it made me think even more about the self-portrait of Douglass and how he wanted to be remembered and the unfinished background in Kollwitz's portrait of the boy and how I don't understand it. Life. I mean do you think Kollwitz left it unfinished because the boy has a lot of living to do?"

"I think it's possible," said David. "You should ask your mom. She would know more than me. She's an art teacher. She would know."

"Well, do you ever think about it?" I asked. "How you want to be remembered one day?"

"It's different when you have kids," said David after slightly hesitating. "You stop thinking about your own mortality and you start putting them first. It's a different ballgame when you have kids. You'll see. When I have to wake up in the morning my first thought is that I cannot waste any time. The time that I waste doesn't put food on the table. The checks I get for each client are real and they're not small and they definitely put food on the table. It's an awesome responsibility. Kids, that is. I guess I don't have much time to think about anything else. I probably should."

12

A tow truck with flashing lights slowed up along the curb

behind a stalled car while cabs sped by in the thickening snow. It

was 2:30 P.M. and I floated down the street pulling my jacket

tighter under my chin in a rootless sort of dream. Just for

something to do, I started to scroll through the contacts list in my

phone. There were several friends I thought about calling. Finally,

I called Alex. Alex was going to spend winter break in Detroit, but

I couldn't remember at the time whether he was leaving that day or the next.

"Hey, what's going on?" asked Alex under faint screams of laughter from children in the background.

"Where are you?" I asked.

"Outside the Museum of Contemporary Art," he said, sounding somewhat distracted. "Somehow I was recruited to help my little cousin make a snowman for her class."

"I was going to ask whether you wanted to meet up," I said.

"Why don't you come help?" he asked. "We could use help."

"All right," I said after a slight hesitation.

I quickly flagged down a taxi and stepped inside.

"The Museum of Contemporary Art," I said to the taxi driver.

The driver, a middle-aged man of Asian descent nodded. We drove the length of a block and pulled up to a stop at the light.

"Look at it," he said, pointing to the street. "There is one person crossing at the intersection. It like Sunday night. It Thursday. It holidays. It like Sunday. Everyday like Sunday."

"Has it been slow?" I asked. "Have you noticed a slowdown?"

"Oh, yeah," he said. "Nobody out at night."

He stared out at the street.

"The restaurants are empty, bars are empty, hotels are empty," he said, gesturing. "For sixty dollar you sleep in any hotel. Thirty thousand people supposed to be at convention last week. Three thousand people! Companies save money. Don't send people. Economy is bad, weather is bad."

He ran his hand through his hair.

"It's double trouble," he said.

He paused for a moment.

"Bank of America," he started. "What was Bank of America close at today?"

"I don't know," I said.

"Four dollar," he said.

"Citibank?" he asked. "Two dollar. Two dollar! You know who's doing good? McDonald's. McDonald's doing good. It's cheap, it's clean, and they have good food!"

He looked up at my reflection in the rearview mirror.

"They have hamburgers and salads and chicken sandwiches," he said. "You don't go to McDonald's?"

"No, I do," I said.

"You have family of three—one hundred dollar to go out to dinner," he said. "McDonald's? Twenty to thirty dollars. Sometime you need cheeseburger. Delicious. Sometimes you need hamburger. Delicious. You eat McDonald's everyday, you got problem."

There was a pause.

"This economy is bad, but out of bad comes good," he said. "You learn to save money."

He turned slightly toward me.

"You, like my son, used to get money and spend money," he said. "But now you see neighbor lose job, father lose job—you save money."

He looked out at the street.

"For the younger generation of America, good comes from bad," he said. "You concentrate more. You work harder. You appreciate small things. Am I right?"

"Yeah," I said.

"I have girls in cab," he said. "I ask girls, 'You saving money?' They tell me they are saving money."

He looked at me in the rearview mirror again.

"Smart," he said. "They don't throw money around—waste money like you, like my son, right?"

He cleared his throat.

"They think like a mom," he said. "It's in their nature."

He paused.

"It's like the Queen Bee. It's like what, ah, Tesla said."

He turned slightly toward me again.

"You know Tesla?" he asked. "Nikola Tesla? It's like what he say. Women are going to become the dominant sex in the future. We need to be run by Queen Bees."

13

There were four semi-complete snowmen standing in front of the Museum of Contemporary Art and three other snowmen in varying finality and then the one snowman that Alex was working on, which needed work. There were kids in winter hats, snow pants and tall boots packing snow around its base. Alex had his back to me as he crouched forward to roll what looked like the second snowball.

"It looks like it's coming along," I said.

"It's going to be the best snowman in the whole world," said a little boy.

"What can I do?" I asked Alex, reaching for his hand to shake as he turned around.

"Just start filling in some snow at the bottom of the base," he said, gesturing around the snowman. "It's going to carry some weight, so, I want to make it as wide on the bottom as in the back."

I studied the base of the snowman.

"People only see one side of it anyway," he said. "The front will be round. The front will be nice."

I leaned forward, packing snow along the bottom of the base.

"So what have you been up to since break started?" I asked.

"Not a hell of a lot," he said, rolling the snow of the second ball. "Are you going to see Abigail before she leaves?"

"I don't know," I said, pausing.

"You probably should with everything that's been going on," he urged.

I leaned forward and packed more snow around the bottom of the base.

"You want to know something that's confidential?" I asked after a long pause.

"Sure," he said.

"I'm going to quit the debate team."

"You're quitting? Why? Judge Pinegrove?"

"Judge Pinegrove, all of them. All the mini Pinegroves crossing the Rubicon."

Alex had been cut from the debate team the previous year.

"To all the mini Pinegroves crossing the Rubicon," he said, lifting a fake drink in an empty hand into the air in a ceremonial toast.

I lifted a fake drink in an empty hand half-way in the air.

He turned back to the snowball and continued rolling it as I smoothed the snow around the base.

"What are you doing for the holidays?" he asked.

"Nothing special," I said. "Just staying around here."

He nodded.

"So you're going to your mom and step-dad's tomorrow, right?" I asked.

"Yep. My childhood friend from up the street is coming too. His parents went on a cruise to the Caribbean this year for Christmas and I didn't think he had anywhere really to go so I invited him for dinner."

He leaned forward, packing the snow together tightly.

"I told him to eat beforehand. My mother is not the greatest cook. As you know, she's Filipino and if you've ever had Filipino cooking, they like their meat overcooked. They think if you overcook it and then add juices it tastes good."

He paused for a moment.

"My step-dad calls it rubber. My older sister is having a friend come for dinner as well and she told her to eat beforehand too. She's twenty-one and she's been through this so many years. She actually jokes about it at the table in front of my mother. My step-dad has no energy left to tell her not to."

I started to square off the back of the base.

"It's funny, my dog won't even eat it," he said. "It's too tough for him to chew."

He laughed to himself.

"He's almost twenty. He's senile and he just lies there all the time. My step-dad says that if he was in the wild he would be dead by now. All he has to do is get up and walk to his dish and eat and go lay back down."

"What is Christmas usually like at your mom's?" I asked.

"It's usually seventy percent desserts, thirty percent main meal in my house," he said. "My mother just goes to Kroger's, which is a Detroit grocery store chain, and buys something like seven pies."

He laughed to himself again.

"But you don't want to have that many desserts," he said. "I kid with my step-dad. I say that he knew he wanted to marry my mom after she said, 'Let me make you a homemade meal.'"

"It was love at first bite," I said.

"Really, I think it was a shot gun wedding," he said. "It was love at first pregnancy test."

I laughed as I finished squaring off the back of the base.

"Do you want to start rolling the third snowball?" he asked.

"Sure," I said.

"The key is to make it a little smaller than the second one," he said. "When you roll it, make sure to end up next to the base so we don't have to carry it too far."

I started packing a snowball. The snow was wet and powdery at the same time, but it packed pretty well.

"After dinner, we usually sit around the TV and let our food digest," he began again, coughing into his arm. "Last year, we watched *It's A Wonderful Life*."

He coughed into his arm again.

"I'm going to make us see it again this year," he said. "It will be the third time I will have seen it over break. Is that wrong?"

I shook my head.

"I love that movie," he said. "I made my step-dad see it for the first time last year and he liked everything except for when it got to the religious stuff. My friend coming this year saw it last year for the first time too and when he saw that it was in black and white he got a little antsy. I think our generation has something against movies in black and white."

I rolled the third snowball toward the base.

"I think my friend has some serious A.D.D. problems though," he said, packing fresh snow on top of the second ball. "Maybe it's just that. Anyway, he told me he liked it. He told me he had always heard about it and that he thought it was going to be different. He said he thought it was going to be worse than it was. That's a compliment coming from him. I asked him, 'Do you think I would choose a bad movie for all of us to watch on the night of Christmas?'"

14

It was 3:00 P.M. and as I walked through the fresh snow

leading to the street, I waved good-bye to the kids, who were now

playing in the snow. I watched as a little snowball fight broke out

and I started to think about how everything seemed to be so much

better when I was their age. I then started to think about Chloe and

how she was doing things that I remembered doing when I was

four. For instance, just last week, I was a witness to her latest

attempt to extend her bedtime. The attempt, itself, mind you, was

very Hoffenberg-esque. I mean, she already had the asking for a snack right at her bedtime down. It helped that my mother was a softie in this department. You see, when it came to asking my mother for food, she could not say no. She could not say no to anyone let alone a four-year-old granddaughter sleeping over for the night on a so-called "vacation at nana's."

"Uncle Cameron!" Chloe had shouted when she first arrived at the apartment. "Uncle Cameron! Uncle Cameron!" She came running to the door.

"What Chloe?" I asked.

"Guess what?" she asked.

"What?" I asked.

"I'm sleeping over," she said. "We're having a sleepover party at Nana's. I'm on vacation! I'm on vacation!"

Later, after dinner, my mother had told me that Chloe could watch fifteen minutes of *The Wizard of Oz* and then she had to go upstairs and have her story and go to bed. This was their ritual.

"Nana?" asked Chloe.

"Yes?" my mother said.

"Um, we forgot, dessert," she said.

"How about some ice cream?" my mother asked.

"Yes, please," Chloe said.

"Uncle Cameron?" my mother started in her best ring leader voice, "would you like some ice cream?"

"Let me see what you have," I said, opening the freezer door.

On the top shelf there was a container of chocolate ice cream and on the middle shelf there was peach ice cream.

"Chloe, do you want chocolate ice cream?" I asked.

"Yes, chocolate!" she said. "Chocolate, chocolate, chocolate," she shouted in varying pitches.

"Ok," I said.

"Ah, Uncle Cameron," started my mom, "let's make it the peach ice cream. Chocolate will keep her up."

"All right," I said.

"With whipped cream?" asked Chloe.

"Ah—," I hesitated.

"We do a little squirt on top," my mom said, gesturing with her hands.

"All right," I said.

I scooped some peach ice cream in a cone for Chloe, squirted a little whipped cream on top and then added three chocolate chips.

"Look what I put on top," I said.

"Chocolate," said Chloe. "Chocolate, chocolate, chocolate."

My mother looked at me.

"Three chocolate chips," I said.

My mother nodded.

The fifteen minutes of *The Wizard of Oz* that Chloe chose started when Dorothy first landed in Oz.

"I like when it is in color," she said.

I sat there watching Chloe lick her ice cream cone as much as I was watching the movie. She was taking slow, small licks just like a pro. Fifteen minutes? I could see from the way she would look around the room that she was going to extend those fifteen minutes by anyway possible. My mother didn't catch it. I did. But I wrote the Hoffenberg manifesto on how to eat your dessert slowly.

Chloe turned to me when she saw the ruby shoes sticking out from underneath the house and said, "That's the Wicked Witch, but she's not really dead. She comes back when there's smoke."

"Well, Chloe," I said. "That's the Wicked Witch of the West. The Wicked Witch of the East actually is dead. The house killed her when it landed on her."

She looked at me as if lingering in thought. I don't know if she really understood what I was telling her because she then turned around and said, while pointing at the screen, "Those are munchkins!"

"Yes, those are munchkins," I said.

I looked up at the clock above the TV as interested as anybody to see how this was going to play out. When the smoke appeared and the Wicked Witch of the West came running out, Chloe turned to me for reassurance.

"She's just an actor," said Chloe. "She's not a real witch. She's just an actor pretending to be a witch."

It was exactly what my mother had told me when I was her age so that I wouldn't be scared.

"That's right, Chloe," I said. "And when they finish the scene they all go out to lunch together." That was another thing my mother would tell me. That was her line to us growing up. As I looked over at Chloe, it seemed to do the trick because she looked back at the TV and took a couple of small licks from her cone.

It was about two minutes until her fifteen minutes were up when I shouted to my mom, who had stepped into the kitchen to finish the dishes, that Chloe should have three extra minutes because it took me three minutes to select the right scene from the DVD.

"We go until they sing," my mother shouted back over the running water at the kitchen sink as if this was part of the normal routine.

As the Wicked Witch of the West disappeared through a cloud of smoke, Dorothy started singing, "We're off to see the Wizard," and Chloe and my mother, who had come back into the family room at this point, started skipping up the yellow brick road to the upstairs guest bedroom for her bedtime.

"Because, because, because, because, because…," I could hear her off in the distance as she walked up the stairs.

My mother took what was left of Chloe's ice cream cone and gave it to me to put in the freezer for the next day. I remember thinking at that point that Chloe had a lot of learning to do in the old Hoffenberg handbook. It was only when my mother came into the kitchen and put a slice of wheat bread in the toaster with a piece of cheese for an open face toasted cheese about a half-an-hour later that I knew Chloe knew more than I originally thought. She had finished the story my mother had read and now she was asking for her snack after her dessert. It was classic textbook chapter two in the Hoffenberg manifesto.

All she had to say was, "Nana, I'm hungry." Those three words. Those three words were the only three words my mother, the before mentioned softie when it came to snacks at any time of day or night for her children or grandchildren, could not say no to.

I kind of laughed as I watched my mother stand over the toaster. My mother went upstairs with the toasted cheese and read Chloe another story and finally told her, when she realized Chloe was eating the crust of the bread nibble by nibble, that she had five minutes to finish it and whatever she didn't finish would be put into the refrigerator for the next day. I heard later that, at that point, Chloe proceeded to devour it and when my mother had finished the second story a couple of minutes after that, Chloe asked whether she could say goodnight to me. It would have been her third time saying goodnight to me and my mother, looking tired at this point, put the old kibosh on that idea and some time over the next fifteen minutes they both fell asleep in bed together.

I glanced at my watch. It was 3:25 P.M. On the corner, I took out my napkin and negotiated the word, *"Good Uncle,"* on it. It was the sixth word. I then turned the corner and walked down the street wondering whether there was someone else I could call as I slowed to a virtual stop. It was the unmistakable bobbing of

Dolan's stupendous hair through the glass window that had first

caught my eye. Then it was the toothy smile.

15

I can't tell you that I was surprised to see Dolan eating at an expensive restaurant after having anticipated it, but I think actually seeing him there with a medium rare fillet buttered for the gods made an impression on me nonetheless. As I pulled myself level to the restaurant window, I watched in silence. God was he chomping. It was very Galeckian, this chomping.

Over his shoulder a news report flashed on the TV at the bar. I stood reading the closed captions. They were telling people to throw out their bags of spinach because of a multi-state E. Coli breakout. Right when they reported it I looked over at the near

empty dish of creamed spinach on the table in front of Dolan. I

looked back over at the TV and when I started to think about the

spinach salad I had eaten at the Better Business Club luncheon I

began to feel sick. The reporter said that that you could get

diarrhea, kidney failure or death if you contracted E. Coli. So now

I thought I was going to get E. Coli and die. A girl in Michigan had

already died from it and a number of other people were sick.

The reporter said that it was thought to have been caused by a

flood that soaked animal feces into the ground where the spinach

was growing. He said if the animal feces soaks into the ground, it

soaks into the spinach roots too and then it won't wash off when

you rinse it under water because it grows inside the spinach leaves.

They showed a crappy animation to illustrate the animal feces

soaking into the roots of the spinach and then how it grows inside

the spinach leaf and, to tell you the truth, I started to gag. I was

already picturing it growing in my stomach and attacking my blood

cells.

They said restaurants were being forced to change their menus and grocery stores were taking the bags off of their shelves. Then they showed some footage of some doofus produce worker at some local grocery store throwing away bags of spinach. It was some really interesting footage they were showing us of this doofus produce worker I will tell you, but it scared the hell out of me. How would you know if you had kidney failure?

I don't think I ever heard of someone calling their doctor and complaining about kidney failure. I could almost picture my tombstone and it saying I died from eating a spinach salad at some twelve person Better Business Club luncheon. In all honesty, I don't think anyone would cry about someone dying like that. I really think that if I died that way, people would just say, "What an unlucky bastard."

Across the street, a homeless man and woman who looked like they had been frozen out of an alley were standing beside a garbage can. The man leaned over inside and started looking for something interesting while the woman stood there watching. I felt a shiver from the wind off the lake and I suddenly started to wonder what they would be doing during the night. The homeless man took his head out of the garbage can long enough to ask a man in a gray scarf waiting for his car at the corner for his leftovers.

"I'm not a bad man," said the homeless man after no response. "We're not bad people," he said, referring to himself and the woman.

As the homeless couple turned away to the street, a man in a blue hat who had been standing by the door of the restaurant with his teenaged daughter watching the homeless couple while waiting for his car came over with his doggy bag from the restaurant and handed it to the homeless man.

"It's a fillet and garlic mashed potatoes," said the man in the blue hat.

"Bless you," said the homeless man. The woman let out a primal shriek.

The man in the blue hat nodded and as he turned around, I noticed that he had dropped one of his gloves on the ground.

Without thought, I hurried down the street, picked it up, and ran after him before he got into his car.

"Sir!" I yelled. "Sir!"

The man in the blue hat paid the valet, stopped and turned toward me. His daughter was looking at me from the front seat of the car.

"You dropped your glove," I said.

"Oh, thank you," he said, checking his pockets. "Thank you very much," he said again, taking it from me and smiling.

I turned away and as I walked up the street, I saw the homeless couple eating the steak with their hands. They were eating it so fast I don't know if they were even tasting it. As I walked up the street, I sent a text to Galecki to see where he was. I kind of wanted to know if anything else happened at the holiday party after I had left.

16

Up the block through a crack in the blinds I could see a silhouette of a woman standing in the window of a massage salon. As I pressed up against the window to get a better look, the first thing I thought was that she looked a lot like a young Demi Moore. A young Demi Moore! I couldn't believe that I actually had said that. I realized at that moment that I was becoming more and more like my mother. I have an uncanny memory of my mother once telling a waiter at a restaurant, "You look like a young Cary Grant," when our waiter looked nothing like a young Cary Grant.

I sat there at the time like, "Ah, can we get some more bread Young Cary Grant?" In an effort not to be over critical, I think my mother was in somewhat of a cocoon at the time from watching old movies with my Grandma Gertrude, who had Alzheimer's. She had been trying to use the movies to spark my grandma's memories, but she was fighting an uphill battle against science and all it did was leave images of old movie stars on the tongue of her lips and lead her to make comments such as the Cary Grant one.

Anyway, after a slight hesitation, I turned toward the door of the massage salon and went in.

"Can I help you?" the young Demi Moore asked.

"How much is a massage?" I asked in a deep voice.

"Sixty dollars for an hour," she said, as she ran a hand through her hair.

"Sixty dollars?"

I stood there silently in thought.

"We can do $30 for a half hour if you'd like," she said.

"All right," I said after a pause.

She requested I sign a waiver that held the salon not liable for any injuries I may incur from the massage.

"It's a standard form we have everyone sign," she said, handing it to me.

I read the first couple of sentences with her watching me and then skimmed the rest of it and signed it. I then handed her my fake driver's license. It was an old license from a neighborhood friend, Alan Rubenstein, who was a sophomore at Illinois. He didn't look anything like me, but it worked.

"Ok, now, Alan, let's head into the back to a room," she said very upbeat.

I started to follow her.

"I'm Paige, by the way," she said, offering her hand. "Have you had a massage before?"

"Actually, this is going to be my first time," I said.

"Great," she said with a smile. "My second newbie of the day."

I nodded.

"Well, because you're a newbie, I'm going to tell you how we're going to do it," she said. "You're going to undress down to your boxers, climb onto the table and lie down flat on your stomach under the sheet."

I looked over at the table and the sheet.

"There's a hook for your clothes," she said, pointing to a hook in the wall above a chair in the middle of the room. "I'm going to close the door to give you some privacy and I'm going to give you about five minutes while I finish up something in the front and then I'll be in."

"All right," I said, nodding.

She smiled and went out of the room, closing the door behind her. I quickly undressed to my boxers and stiffly leaned forward across the table under the sheet. A few minutes later, I heard a knock at the door.

"Ready?" asked Paige, slowly poking her head into the room.

"Yeah," I said.

I could hear her come over to the table. I listened to the music in the background as she started rubbing my shoulders in a circular motion.

"Let me know if I'm being too hard," she said.

I nodded sideways on the table.

"Do you clench your teeth?" she asked.

"Um, maybe," I asked.

"Has your dentist ever told you that you clench your teeth?" she asked.

"I think I do sometimes," I said. "I think I do it in my sleep."

"You know, clenching your teeth actually tightens the muscles around your neck. Does this hurt?"

"A little."

"I can tell. The muscles on your neck are out a little bit."

Her hands moved around the tops of my shoulders.

"It's not like you look like a duck or anything. I mean I can only see it because I'm standing right over you staring very closely at your neck."

She paused for a moment.

"But, that can cause some discomfort. My dad clenches his teeth. That's how I know."

I nodded again.

"So are you going anywhere for Christmas?" she asked after several moments of silence.

"No," I said. "What about you?"

"No," she said. "I'm boring too."

She laughed loudly.

"I went home for Thanksgiving though," she said. "It was funny, my parents, don't get me wrong I love them to death, but only my parents would decide to clean out the storage closet over Thanksgiving."

"Cheap labor," I said.

"Yeah, really, right?" she said. "And the storage closet is a good size closet and it has a lot of junk."

She laughed to herself.

"It has all the centerpieces for the church. My mother is in charge of all the meals at the church and she has the Easter centerpieces sitting there and the Christmas centerpieces."

She paused for a moment.

"She uses the same centerpieces every year. She also does the meals at the funerals. She usually uses flowers donated from the mortuary."

I could feel her hands moving down my back.

"The mortuary will usually call and have flowers to donate and my mom usually picks them up and then uses them as the centerpieces for the meals at the funerals. The mortuary sometimes donates it to the hospital."

She paused for a moment.

"The hospital is across the street. I know, great thing to see when you look out the window of the hospital—a graveyard."

She laughed in a subtle way.

"Anyway, sometimes the mortuary donates flowers to the hospital and sometimes they will call my mom up and donate them to her and my mom never wants to tell them no or that she doesn't need them because she doesn't want them to stop calling so she always goes and picks them up whether there is a funeral or not and when there is no funeral she will just decorate the house with them."

She paused.

"So, over Thanksgiving, we had our house decorated with lilies. Lilies were everywhere around the house."

She took a short breath.

"Of course, she doesn't tell them that she decorated the house. She just doesn't want them to stop calling."

She laughed to herself.

"So, over Thanksgiving, they called I think twice and I was the one asked to go pick the flowers up."

There was silence for a moment.

"Can I ask you something?" I asked.

"Sure," she said.

She started working on my right side.

"I know this is kind of strange, but I want to get your thoughts on something," I said.

"Ok," she said in an intrigued way.

"I was at the Art Institute earlier today and I saw a self-portrait of Frederick Douglass and I started wondering how he wanted to be remembered and it made me realize that I didn't know how I wanted to be remembered," I said. "Now, Frederick Douglass had a very stern look on his face and he knew that was how he was going to be remembered. If I were to ask you, would you have any idea how you want to be remembered?"

"Hmm," she said in a thoughtful pause. "Tough question."

She paused for another moment.

"I don't know," she finally said. "I think I would be smiling in my picture. I would smile, not laugh like ha ha, but smile."

"So you would want people to know you are happy?" I asked.

"A smile doesn't always mean happiness," she said. "For instance, I was in Thailand last year and everyone smiles in

Thailand. And they're not all really happy. It's supposed to be cool and even keel."

As I nodded, my phone started vibrating.

"Do you need to check to see who it is?" she asked.

"Yeah, probably," I said.

She reached for my phone in my pants pocket, which was dangling from the hook, and handed it to me. It was Galecki.

"I should probably quickly answer it," I said after a hesitation.

"Can I call you back?" I quickly said as I answered the phone.

"Cameron!" Galecki shouted. "Please tell me you can come pick me up."

"What?" I asked. "Is everything all right?"

"No!" he said in a vague panic. "I lost my wallet."

"You what?" I asked.

"It's a long story," he said. "I need you to hop in a cab right now and come pick me up on the corner of Delaware and Dearborn."

17

As I sat back against the seat looking out the window at a passing blur of whitenesss, the cab crossed Delaware Street and pulled through the intersection of Chestnut and State.

"There he is!" I shouted, pointing to Galecki, who was becoming more visible on the corner.

The headlights of the cab flashed on him.

"Oh God, Oh God! Right here!" I mumbled when I realized he was only wearing boxers and a winter coat.

He was hopping up and down barefoot on the frosted pavement to stay warm, his coat hugging his pink flabby drumstick-like bare legs about mid-thigh.

"Christ! It's fuckin' cold outside!" he yelled as he hurled himself convulsively into the backseat of the cab.

"Well, you're not wearing any pants!" I shouted, facing him.

He sat there in profile, on the seat without pants, filling his half of the backseat to the very brim. I scooted across the seat to make more room for his spilled over plumpness. His glasses immediately fogged up. He quickly took them off, exposing an indented, fleshy "V" on the bridge of his nose. As he held them in one hand, he started to blow on his closed fists to warm up his fingers. He then rubbed his pink flabby bare legs with those same closed fists.

"I only had time to grab my coat," he said with quivering lips.

He turned half toward me, looking blindly about the backseat. It was an embarrassingly intense moment. I noticed that he was attempting to sink down in his seat, but there was no sinking.

"You didn't tell me you didn't have any pants on," I said as I broke into a short laugh.

"I didn't think I would have to," he said.

"What happened?" I asked.

Galecki rubbed his thighs again to warm them and then started to wave his glasses back and forth above his head. When the fog remained on the glass, he started to blow on them.

"If I were to tell you what actually happened, you'd never believe me," he said.

Galecki went on to tell me, as I confirmed at a later time, a semi-true story of how he and the Ice Princess had left the party together and how when they went back to her parents' apartment her boyfriend came over unexpectedly and Galecki had to climb down the fire escape half-dressed. Quite honestly, I don't think I would have ever believed him if I hadn't seen it with my own eyes.

The cab pulled up to the curb in front of Galecki's parents' building on Lakeshore Drive. Galecki ran from the cab into the building where the doorman met him with a slight smile. As I sat there a moment watching Galecki walk barefoot through the lobby, I scribbled on the primavera-stained napkin, *Good Friend.* I then told the cab driver to take me to Park West and Dickens Street. Abigail was probably packing for her trip.

18

The cab pulled across the traffic along Park West to the west side of the street. I paid the driver and got out and walked into the warm entrance of Abigail's parents' building. The doorman let me right up. He called the elevator and everything. As the doors closed, I stood silently and listened to the same instrumental version of *The Girl From Ipanema* that I had heard so many times before in the same elevator. You'd think they wouldn't play the same song all the time.

The doors opened on the twelfth floor and as I walked down the hallway, Mrs. Fleming was waiting.

"Hi, Cameron," she said. "What a pleasant surprise."

"Hi, Mrs. Fleming," I said. "I wanted to see Abigail before she, um, before all of you left for break."

"Well, I know she'd love to see you," she said. "She'll be home any minute now from dance class."

I nodded.

"Excuse me a second, hon," she started. "I need to check the chicken."

She walked from the hallway into the kitchen while I followed slowly behind. As she opened the oven door, steam escaped in rushed white clouds.

"I'm making chicken Madeira tonight," she said over her shoulder as she bent down to grab hold of the tray. "It's a new recipe. Why don't you stay for dinner?"

Through the smells of the chicken Madeira, she straightened, holding the tray firmly in both hands with a smile as if she was relieved she hadn't burned it.

"Ok, hon?" she said, turning toward the table.

As she placed the tray on warmers, I looked over and saw that there were four chairs around the table and three place settings and the only thing that I could think about was that there would have been four place settings if Abigail's younger sister Katie had not died and that the fourth chair should be for Katie, not for me, and how unfair it was that Katie was dead because she didn't deserve to be and how Mrs. Fleming didn't have a gallbladder and neither did Abigail and, all of a sudden, all I could do was—I had to leave.

"Mrs. Fleming," I said. "You know what? I can't. I forgot. I don't know how I forgot about this, but you know how I'm on the debate team at school?"

She nodded.

"Well, we're going to Thailand," I said. "Tomorrow afternoon—but I got things that I need to do by morning."

It was a terrible excuse, but I couldn't immediately think of anything else at the time.

"We're in this tournament and we're going up against this other high school from Bangkok," I said.

She stood there looking at me silently.

"I've heard it's an interesting country," she finally said.

"Me too," I said. "You know, a smile there doesn't always mean happiness. I mean, I've heard that everyone there smiles. And they're not all really happy. It's supposed to be cool and even keel."

She nodded.

"Anyway, I got to go," I said. "You know, because of Thailand."

I then turned around quickly and left.

19

As I stumbled along the uneven drift along the sidewalk, the silence of the snow was deafening. My nose started dripping and my eyes started to tear from the wind fresh off the lake. As I slogged under the viaduct leading into Lincoln Park, almost falling, I could hear the cars whizzing past me on the street above. The park benches lining the path were layered with snow. A man and a woman holding hands walked swiftly in front of me and then glided a few feet across the snow on the heels of their shoes as if they were wearing skates. They did it again around the bend as a dog approached.

"He's friendly," said the owner, a beaten up old woman with a blue knit hat on her head. "He was abused. He's from the shelter. He just doesn't like anything swinging."

She pointed toward the man and woman.

"Like your arms," she said. "How your arms were swinging."

She paused.

"He didn't like that," she said.

Smoke from my breath punched out as I listened to the squawking birds above. They were unseen, only heard. As I walked along a small path, it was easier to walk in the broken snow of the footprints before me rather than the slope alongside. As I walked step for step in those unknown footprints, I started to think about Marty Feldman and what made him feel like he had The Golden Handcuffs. I don't know why I was thinking about that, but I was. Then I started to think about Wayne. Why did Wayne react the way he did when he won twelve dollars in a twelve person raffle he presided over?

I then started to think about how sentimental Todd Barrett got about high school at the Art Institute and how the cab driver taking me to the Museum of Contemporary Art said that women were going to be the dominant sex in the future. I thought about the boy from the video with the amputated leg sledding around the ice rink at the park district, how David Adelman said when he wakes up in the morning he can't waste time because he has to put food on the table, and how Eric dressed up as Santa Claus for second and third graders at a Christmas Festival at Daley Plaza. I started to think about how Miguel was going to Spain to spread the word of Jesus, how Dolan was sitting in an expensive restaurant eating a fillet buttered for the Gods while outside a homeless man lowered his head inside a garbage can looking for something interesting, and how James Abernathy had been killed in a foxhole in New Guinea by a shell in WWII when he was eighteen years old. Then, for some reason, I thought about Judge Pinegrove and how he would yell "Like Caesar Crossing the Rubicon!" with the look of Almighty God in his eyes before every debate tournament.

I started to think about Paige at the massage salon. I thought about her mother and how she would pick flowers up from the mortuary and if there was no funeral to donate them to she would just decorate her own house with them. I started to think about Alex and how he said his mother made a traditional Filipino dinner for Christmas every year and overcooked the meat and added juices.

As my mind drifted, I started to think about my Grandma Gertrude and how over the years her memory had slowly been taken from her by Alzheimer's. I then started to think about Abigail and how her mother was convinced she had to have her gallbladder removed after she complained of stomachaches.

At that point, I started to think about Arnie Schneiderman of all people. Arnie Schneiderman! Why did Arnie Schneiderman almost kill himself reaching over the table and the silverware for Dolan's hand that night at the beginning of the Internship Program? My thoughts then started to drift to Galecki. How could Galecki ever have left the party with The Ice Princess? What about the guy in the blazer rolling up the red carpet? Did he know that he was going to be rolling up the red carpet in the fake photo shoot when he woke up in the morning? What about the woman sitting in the horse carriage? How long did she have to sit there and smell the horse's ass until someone wanted a ride? Did anyone else think the guy dressed up as a Chocolate Peanut Butter Cup looked like a child molester with the way the tongue was stapled to his costume and his maniacal grin? Was the old man with the bushy gray hair who was playing the grand piano at Macy's on State Street shutting his eyes to be closer to the music or farther? Why did my father one day jump from a stool with a rope tied around his neck and his knees knowingly bent so they wouldn't drag along the floor? Why did Old Man Russell have to look so old and lonely and miserable with his pork chop sideburns? Where was the Crab Lady, Cane Man, Old Lady Lemon Fingers, Cornrows and Pillow Head?

The swan pond at the zoo was iced over and covered in snow. The boathouse with the paddleboats was locked up. There were no animals outside by the barnyard, but a slight hint of a lingering smell was still there. As I passed by Café Brauer and looked closely at the long ice crystals forming on the awning of the Ice Cream Shoppe, I thought about Chloe and how she had said that the ice cream shop gets its ice cream from God.

As I rounded a south facing snow slope, there was a boy sledding. I could hear him yelling and laughing as he went down the incline. His father was standing on top of the slope watching. I stood and watched and I started to think about my father and my childhood and after a short while I walked over and asked the father if I could go down the slope one time on the other sled. There was another sled abandoned off to the side on top of the slope and the father looked me over for a second.

"It's pretty slick over the ridge," he said, finally.

"Ok," I said. "I'll go slow."

He gestured for me to go ahead.

I sat down onto the sled. Clenching my teeth, I nudged it forward. The boy looked at me as if I was out of my mind. I nudged it forward a little more and as it broke the plain it hurtled down the slope. I let out a loud boyish yell for the slope gods. The wind hit my face and shot my hair back, and as the sled slowed to a stop at the bottom, I looked up the slope and the father and the boy were looking down at me from the top and the boy was still giving me a look as if I was crazy. I got up and started to walk up the slope with the sled under my arm.

"It was pretty slick right over that ridge, wasn't it?" asked the father.

"Yeah," I said. "It really picked up right at that point." I took a breath. "Um, would you mind if I did it one more time?"

"Go ahead," the father said. "Have at it."

I smiled and put the sled down on the top of the slope. The boy stood there looking at me. He just stood there not saying anything.

"I used to go sledding with my father when I was about your age," I said to the boy. "It's been awhile."

I sat down onto the sled and got my feet tucked into place.

"You go first," I said to the boy. "I'll wait."

The boy climbed into his sled and inched it to the edge of the slope and went down. He yelled again as it sped down and at the bottom it tipped over and he fell into the snow. He was laughing as he laid there. He then started making a snow angel on his back.

I inched my sled to the edge and started down. My hair shot back and the wind hit my face. As it sped down to the bottom, just like with the boy, it tipped over and dropped me into the snow. After I made sure I didn't break anything, I started to make a snow angel too—right there next to the boy. The boy started to laugh, and as I looked up, I saw the father standing on top of the slope. It was a short slope and he wasn't far away, but I guess the light was fading down the horizon behind him because as I looked up I could only see him looking down on us in a silhouette. The image had an immediately deeper meaning. I fought with myself for a moment— then I suddenly broke down in an open, silent scream. I cried upwards into the cold air. It was really coming out. I just couldn't suppress it anymore, I guess. I cried about my father. I cried about not having the chance to say goodbye. I cried for the end of my

innocence. The boy of my childhood was gone forever and so was

his father. It just all started coming out. I couldn't cry at the

funeral, but just leave it to me to cry like a bastard that day looking

up from the snow at the silhouette. I stood up and began collecting

myself.

As I started walking away, I felt different. I felt better. I took

my gloves off and stuffed them into my coat pockets and smeared

the tears from my cheeks with the back of my hand, and as I

steered along the curve of the path, I realized I was starting to get

to know myself. It wasn't until I had put my hands back into my

coat pockets to reach for my gloves that I realized the napkin with

the primavera splotch and the attributes was gone. For a moment, I

contemplated going back to the slope and looking for it, but as I

stood there thinking about how I wanted to be remembered one

day, suddenly I realized I didn't need it anymore. What I needed

was time—time to get to know myself. I was like the boy in

Kollwitz's painting. This is what I started to think as I stood there.

Just like the boy in Kollwitz's painting, I needed my background to fill in.

A soft snowflake drifted down and landed on my nose. As I looked up, it had begun to snow again. I watched the sky glittering with snowflakes and the ground sparkling with the drift. I thought about the plight of each flake as it fell to a new life and a new peace. I stood there sharing in the beautiful silence with the trees, and then I slogged across a sheet of glazed ice, leaving the list behind as if it were a sacrificial offering to the slope gods.

"See this building right over here?" said a man holding his daughter up over his head on his shoulders. "We're going in there. There's a bathroom in there."

The moon was dim, but looming and getting brighter in the distance. I stood in the twilight of the coming night. There was a little souvenir stand outside the Lion House selling stuffed animals, magnets and other trinkets. Powered by a new sense of understanding about myself, I wanted to get something for Chloe to give to her after the recital. I started to look through the rack of stuffed animals for one that had a smile and as I stood there I started to think back about Paige and how she had told me everyone smiles in Thailand, but not everyone is happy. I guess that was how I was starting to feel about life because even though each of the stuffed animals on the rack appeared to be smiling, none of them seemed happy to me and I wanted one that looked happy.

"They all look indifferent," I said to the sales clerk, pointing to the seam along the mouth of one of the stuffed animals. "Their smiles."

"There are more inside the Lion House," the sales clerk said with an expressionless face, pointing.

I walked inside the Lion House and I started looking at each of the faces of the stuffed animal lions until I found one that looked just right. It was the only one that looked happy in the entire bunch. It was eight dollars. I bought it and as I walked through the Lion House toward the far end, I tore off the sales tag from its ear. As I stared at its smile, over my shoulder there was an actual lion yawning on a bed of steep rocks behind a cage. He had

a blank stare on his face. I stared at him for a moment and he

stared at me. I looked down at the stuffed animal in my hand and

then back over at him and wondered what he could possibly be

thinking about while he looked at me.

There was a sign next to the cage that said his name was

William and that he was from Africa. The tiger in the neighboring

cage was pacing back and forth. He looked as restless as I had been

feeling all day. The sign next to his cage said that his name was

Seymour and that he was from India. I looked over at him and I

thought about how William, Seymour and I had all made our long

journeys to this place and how at that exact moment, we were all

there together.

Outside on the steps leading up to the Lion House an ice

sculptor was sculpting a large block of ice into a swan. I stood

there and watched as chips of ice speckled the early night air. The

neck and the head of the swan had already been delicately

sculpted. It was the body that had yet to emerge. I glanced at my watch and quickly started looking for a cab amid the flashing

headlights out on Park West when I realized I was going to be late

for Chloe's recital.

The stillness of the school in the falling darkness was in

sharp conflict with the sheens of bright light in the parking lot and

the upbeat, smiling faces of the entering crowd of parents who had

come from around the city with anticipation. I walked through the

school following the shuffling feet in front of me and lingering

clatter to the auditorium.

There was a background of white snow like hills in the

distance and a big Christmas tree with colored ornaments and

scattered boxes of presents rising perpendicular to a small, wooden

sleigh. A sea of stationary heads and faces were already settled in

their seats and waiting for something to happen in the same way

Henry Miller had meant it. My mother and everyone else were

somewhere near the front of the stage saving a seat for me. I

looked row by row for them following a loud roar from the crowd as the overhead house lights turned down. Unannounced, bunches of shy, little girls in white tutu's came out onto the stage in a long, unbroken line like tiny future Rockettes. I stood there placidly watchful a moment looking for Chloe before finally sitting down in an empty seat along the aisle after a few prodding loud noises from the throat of the woman in the row behind me.

As I sat back in my chair holding the little lion stuffed animal in my hands, I looked up at the stage and then at the gleeful expressions and loud voices around me.

They weren't waiting for something to happen, I started to think to myself.

It was only then I realized that something already had happened.

A repeat of innocence! I thought.

The momentum of the thought persisted and as the spotlights shined brightly on the stage, I watched axioms in a mirror image stole around the crowd, eagerly polishing the last of the sentimental dust from its long ago forgotteness.

Chloe stood near the sleigh slightly stooped with her head forward nervously holding the charm on her necklace in her fingers. She looked down from the stage in a fixed stare directed into the shadows of the audience. When the music began, the line of little girls threw their arms into the air in a start and began pecking at the stage with their toes. Apart from them, Chloe stood there as if searching. Under a stir of voices, I stood and waved and smiled and Chloe saw me and it was as if that was what she was waiting for because she quickly turned and joined the other little girls in the next twirl as if she hadn't missed a beat.

www.ingramcontent.com/pod-product-compliance
Lightning Source LLC
Chambersburg PA
CBHW050946120626
46552CB00001B/409